A Grave Business

A Grave Business

ALAN HORSFIELD

EJH
TALENT
PROMOTION

First published in Australia in 2016

Requests and enquiries should be addressed to:
Alan Horsfield, 9 Milman Drive, Craiglie QLD 4877
anehorsfield@westnet.com.au

National Library of Australia cataloguing in publication data

Creator: Horsfield, Alan, author.
Title: A Grave Business
ISBN: 978-0-9944579-2-9 (paperback)
Subjects: Theft—Juvenile fiction.

Dewey Number: A823.3

Edited by Rosemary Peers
Cover and internal illustrations by Nancy Bevington
Internal design and layout by DiZign Pty Ltd, Sydney

Printed in Australia

The words of the first verse of 'Basin Street Blues'

Won't you come along with me,
To the Mississippi,
We'll take a boat to the land of dreams,
Steaming down the river to New Orleans.

From 'Basin Street Blues' (1926)
by Spenser Williams (1889–1965)

CHAPTER 1

'*Then I tap-dance the Louisiana blues*
With cans clipped onto my Nike shoes.'

LOUISIANA, EARLY '90s

In Nawlins—or New Orleans, if you prefer—the dead are 'buried' in crypts above the ground. Sometimes the living can end up there too. I should know.

My dad sits on a crate in Royal Street, in the French Quarter, as we wait for the crowd to become more than a sprinkling of early morning workers going into local shops.

'Should limber up a bit,' my dad says. 'You're not the only kids on the street.'

He means get in some practice—now.

Kids! I look at Lincoln and roll my eyes. I hate practising our routine when there is no one much to watch. Dad reckons it's the entertainer in me! Lately I haven't been too sure about doing it in front of some spectators.

1

Linc, on the other hand, can really tap. He has feet that simply zing when he gets going. It's like listening to drums played by an expert. And watching a real pro. Feet and legs go like long, loose drumsticks. Hips like they were trimmed especially for tapping. Girls stop and watch. Eyelids flutter. Beat out dat rhythm, as they say!

Other kids play instruments or just hang out every Saturday and school hols. Except maybe the Neville brothers, but that's another matter. Don't tangle with those hoods!

The summer's break is a break for us—a break from school, not from work.

We have to come across from Algiers on the Canal Street ferry—they don't charge pedestrians, just the cars— and tap-dance for the tourists. No matter what the weather.

With a bit of luck they'll put a few notes in Dad's tip-tin and he'll share it out at the end of the day. Twenty-five per cent for me—Xavier Samson. Twenty-five per cent for my partner, Lincoln Jones. And the rest—fifty per cent!—for my dad, Dizzy Samson. They call him Dizzy after some old Nawlins jazzman. And what does Dad do for his fifty per cent? He looks after the tip-tin and us—protects us. So he says!

Could have used a bit of protection later on, as it turned out.

'More people on Bourbon Street,' complains Linc as Dad hits the PLAY button on the tape recorder. We always start with 'When the Saints Go Marching In'. It's corny but Dad reckons it's what makes the tourists part with their money.

'Not as much money. People on Royal have the big bucks. They're eating in class restaurants. They're shopping for class goods.' Dad sits on his crate near the tip-tin. He's been around a long time and seen a lot of changes—almost a Nawlins character.

I shrug. Could be right. The tourists here aren't into partying all night as much as they are on Bourbon. And the shops are mostly antique shops and pricey fashion stores. Not many places selling plastic voodoo junk and cheap, last-year's Jazz Festival T-shirts.

About ten o'clock we're having a bit of a break when a dirty, red pick-up pulls up outside the New Orleans Genuine Antique Store across the street.

Linc and I watch as two men unload a few, very dirty cartons and carry them into the shop.

'Looks pretty heavy Xavier,' says Linc, real serious but without much interest.

'Bet it's something made of silver, or something precious. Or the latest antiques for the tourists!' grumbles Dad without looking up from counting his, correction, *our* money. 'Not much here today!'

All that tapping for practically nothing. I'd be better off selling plastic sunshades to the tourists. Or fake voodoo dolls—pins extra!

We do a few more sets before lunch by which time Dad has got bored, or hungry. 'I'm off,' Dad says suddenly, as if he's just had a great idea. 'Coming?'

I turn to Linc and then I say, 'Naw. Think we'll go down to Jackson Square and watch some of the bands.'

'Ain't no bands down there! Just a few burnt out musos playing for pennies—or peanuts. Crowds treat 'em like circus monkeys. Like they are still in the 1890s, not the 1990s!'

Dad's probably right but I really enjoy watching the old guy play a string bass that has only three strings. Wouldn't see it anywhere else 'cept in the French Quarter in Nawlins, I reckon.

'Reckon Louis Armstrong used to play there,' says Linc.

'Hey Dad, how about some of our money?' I cry, as he starts to push it into his jacket pocket.

He squints at me sideways, rubbing his wrinkled, stubbled face before giving a shrug and handing Linc and me ten bucks each. 'Don't go throwing it at buskers,' he growls as he turns and takes out his cell phone.

'No way,' I reply quietly. 'This is my hard-earned cash.' I'm not any different from most other people in the street!

Linc and I cross the street in front of the New Orleans Genuine Antique Store. I pause for a second to look at my shadowy reflection in the clean, glass shopwindow.

I'm pretty good-looking for a young street entertainer. My hair's black and short but not shaved. I have a good trim body but I'm not thin, unless you listen to Mama complain. Good body for tap dancing, I smile to myself.

'Then I tap-dance the Louisiana blues
With cans clipped onto my Nike shoes.'

But Linc is frowning. 'Hey, you remember all those cartons full of gold and silver and stuff. Not true! I can see the men inside unpacking them. Bits of old stone ornaments and blocks—or something.'

I have no idea why people would waste good money on old stone ornaments—not really interested. Too busy trying to study my side profile in the glary window.

Suddenly one of the men looks up. Annoyance flashes across his face. He says something to the other guy before he raises his fist and roars at us. 'Clear off you two!'

Linc is taken by surprise by the aggro outburst and doesn't move for a moment or two but I'm a survivor.

'Wouldn't catch me buying dirty junk like that!' I call over my shoulder as I duck past the door and head down the street. I like to be on the move.

It doesn't take Linc long to catch up.

'Big mouth,' he huffs.

Linc doesn't appreciate my fine verbal wit.

CHAPTER 2

When I get home that night Dad is in the corner of the sitting room on his laptop. Dad calls it his computer. He's just got a copy of a program for songwriting. Mama is in our small kitchen preparing some gumbo for our evening meal.

'Any emails for me?' I call. I don't get any so I didn't expect an answer.

Dad growls, 'Not unless you have a friend called Peter Moore.'

I told him I didn't have any friends called Peter Moore or even Peter Rabbit. Don't know anyone called Peter Moore.

'Well, he keeps sending us emails with attachments. And they are not for me!'

'Might be spam? How many has he sent?' I say as I go over and stand beside him.

'Two, that I can remember.'

'Did you open the attachments?'

Dad being a practical and basically honest man says, 'Tweren't for me.'

I have a bit more curiosity than that. I would have opened them right away. I don't worry too much about viruses. But I don't say anything. Dad will let me have a play on his machine later.

'Want me to send this one back to where it came from?' I ask as casually as I can.

'Might as well. Might be important. Who knows with these things nowadays?

Dad gets up from his wooden chair and leaves the room to watch TV. He won't even give me a second glance once the basketball comes on unless he loses the picture again. Our set is very ancient.

I check the email. It's a pretty short message. I read the information at the top of the page. I notice it is using a strange Louisiana server. Subject: Hot Goods. And it was definitely sent to our email address—Samson.

Hello Winnie, Thought you might comment on the attached ad. Like to know what you think of the pricing. Too cheap?

Hope you received the earlier message. Please confirm you have carefully read this one. Peter

I glance towards Dad as I open the attachment. He's fully absorbed in the match.

The attachment is a bit odd. Just pictures of lots of old furniture and a few old kettles and things. In the middle of the page is a frame with the words 'Most goods 25% off for cash', but the prices are anything but cheap!

I close the attachment and hit the REPLY button. I key in a short message: 'Not for Samson.' Then I hit SEND.

Maybe not a smart thing to do.

'Done that Dad,' I call a bit louder than the TV. He is concentrating real hard because the picture is starting to rock and roll. Well, roll anyway.

'Good. Don't like keeping other people's personal mail.'

Dad has never realised that returning mail doesn't mean you send back the original message. You send a copy. The original is still on the machine. For some reason, probably laziness, I don't trash the message. I keep it and the attachment on the machine.

Lucky for me, or maybe unlucky, I will later have another look at the attachment.

Right now I do a FIND 'Hot Goods' for the earlier message.

The machine finds the other email and it too has an attachment. The message doesn't tell me much and the attachment is just a picture of an angel statue, a very dirty angel statue. Looks to me like it came from a church in ancient Rome or Greece. Who knows?

A message in a frame says: 'Hello Winnie. We could move more of these if we had them. What do you think? Peter.' It looks like the angel's saying it in a speech bubble!

It doesn't get me thinking at all. But then I'm not renowned for my appreciation of sculpture. I wonder who Winnie might be. Some old woman, no doubt.

I close the machine down and go and sit on the arm of the lounge chair Dad's sitting in.

Outside I hear a blast from a paddle-steamer taking tourists up the mighty Mississippi for a moonlight jazz cruise. Some people will spend money on the weirdest things! There's real cheap jazz in Bourbon Street every day. Even cheaper in Jackson Square.

> *'And a Mississippi steamboat floats on by*
> *Full of folks just there for the ride.'*

Who'd buy statues of dirty angels, I wonder vaguely.

CHAPTER 3

Next day before we leave for the French Quarter and our favourite pastime I show Linc the two email messages.

'Wonder why they were sent to us?' I say.

'You are probably in his address book,' Linc suggests. 'Some people send their messages to every email address they know.'

I screw up my nose. Doesn't sound sensible to me.

'Maybe it's a virus,' Linc says vaguely.

Linc opens the first attachment—the one with the angel. 'This stuff looks like it's text-box stuff and clip art.' He clicks on the angel's message. The corners of the text box appear on the screen. Linc then drags the text box across the screen.

'Hey, look Xav, there's something under the text box. It looks like a message to someone!'

Peter Moore and Winnie are turning out to be quite a pair of secret communicators.

I push in closer. There's a second message under the top message. 'Might be a secret message,' I say hopefully.

'Yair,' agrees Linc with a doubtful snicker.

By now he's dragging the picture of the angel all over the page. Checking for more hidden messages, before I can read anything.

'Nothing under that one!' I say, stating the obvious. I'm even a little bit disappointed.

But Linc's not to be deterred. He opens the latest email attachment from Peter Moore. He clicks on the text and discovers that it too is a text box without a border. He drags it to the right of the page.

'Whoopee,' I chirp. 'More messages!' I can't see anything they say as Linc has started shuffling all the pictures around the page.

'What's this stuff look like to you?' he asks, without looking at me. He's pushing and clicking the mouse like he's been using our machine all his life.

'Old furniture!' I say with a pout and a shrug. Silly question, I think.

'Yair, old furniture!' Linc looks at me as if he has just recognised my genius. 'And where do you get old furniture?'

I know the answer to that. 'In a second-hand furniture store.' I give him a big satisfied grin, like Brer Fox has when he captures Brer Rabbit with a tar baby! Linc just shakes his head in disbelief. I think I'm just about ready to thump him but Dad calls from the yard. 'Ferry's crossing the river now. We got about five minutes.'

He's already outside with his crate and tape recorder and tip-tin.

My sister, Charlotte, and Mama head for the front door. They always see us off.

Linc closes the machine down and we grab our Nikes as we hurry out. The terminal is about five blocks from our house, which is right by the path over the top of the levee.

'Might come over later,' calls Mama as we scramble up the levee bank. She pretends to be the start of an audience if no one is stopping to watch us. Sometimes she puts some coins in our tip-tin hoping that the real tourists will feel obliged to do the same.

Mama makes sure she gets them back when we get home. One tough mama!

In Royal Street we find our place is taken by some fellow who is standing motionless pretending to be the Tin Man out of *The Wizard of Oz*. He's totally painted silver: skin, clothes, hair, shoes, the lot!

What's more annoying is he has this bunch of tourists coming up one by one and having their picture taken with him—then each dropping five dollars into his silver tip-tin! Money for nothing and we have to tap-dance our way to fame and fortune.

Two police officers walk past, giving the Tin Man the once-over with their eyes before turning to cross the street. The younger one is Officer Bell. He's liked around the Quarter because he doesn't come on too strong when there's a bit of trouble.

Next to Mr Tin Man is a woman playing a trumpet with gusto. No one's tossing money into her tip-tin.

Dad pulls at his nose for a few minutes, just watching. I hope he's not thinking of painting me silver!

Linc interrupts my thoughts. 'See that shop across the street? The one where the officers are.'

'Sure, I've seen it! We were near there yesterday,' I snort. I've worked this site for more years than I care to think about.

'You had a good look at it? Read what they have on the window?'

I look towards the shop, momentarily distracted by the two police officers looking in the window. I can't imagine why police officers would want second-hand furniture.

'Well?' asks Linc, as if I'm under interrogation for some unstated crime.

'Sure. New Orleans Genuine Antique Store,' I say without having to read it. I know it off by heart. 'Or do you mean the bakery next door?'

'I mean the New Orleans Genuine Antique Store. Have a closer look at the writing!'

I think Linc's getting exasperated with me. I'm about to look up when the Neville boys go by. The Neville Devils stop and give us a 'Get Lost' look. They're real hustlers. They don't do much real dancing but badger tourists to contribute to their fighting funds.

Nothing like the original Neville brothers he used to know, Dad says often enough. I'm sure these two aren't even distant relations to any real person—maybe gorillas though, that's a thought.

I glare back at the bigger brother, Eustace. He must be nearly seventeen, and weighs half a ton. No wonder Nawlins is called the fat capital of America! I'm thinking I'd like to call him Useless to his face but I'm not quite that brave. He knows I'm mocking him but is not sure how to handle it.

His brother, Lothar, just pouts under hooded eyes. I think he was named after some black comic-book hero. Same shaved head. He has his Nikes hanging over his shoulder so that everyone can see that he has made the caps out of beer cans. He thinks that's real cool.

Dad makes a quick decision. 'Think we'll try Bourbon Street today. Too crowded here!'

That suits Linc and me real fine. We swing our Nikes over our shoulders with our Coke-can taps and follow Dad into St Louis Street. There's much more action in Bourbon Street. Younger crowd.

'Did you see it? What I saw?' demands Linc as we trudge along behind Dad.

'Didn't bother looking. Didn't like their marketing style yesterday!' I snort.

A crowd of young men in cowboy hats come swaggering down St Louis Street and we are forced off the narrow footpath.

Linc sucks in his breath as he drops behind me and says, 'Tell you later.'

'Wow!' I say to myself. 'I can't wait.'

CHAPTER 4

Linc doesn't tell me later.

After we finish for the day and Dad, Mama and Charlotte head off across the river he drags me back to Royal Street.

'Have a look at the sign on the store,' hisses Linc.

I glare at it with mock petulance.

'Read it! Or can't you read?'

I sigh deeply as I silently read the sign.

'So they've been going a long time! So what's so important 'bout that?'

'Read what's on the window!' demands Linc.

I give an exasperated hunch of the shoulders and start to read all the writing on the shopfront a word at a time just to annoy him. 'New – Orleans – Genuine – Antique – Store – and – Collectables – Old – wares – bought – and – sold. – Proprietor – Peter – Moore.' Then it hits me like the kick of a mule that pulls one of them fancy carriages. 'Peter Moore! The guy that sent the emails to some woman.' I give Linc a friendly thump on the shoulder.

Then we look at each other and both have the same idea.

We cross the street and walk up to the shopwindow. It doesn't take us long to recognise a few of the things that were in the email attachment.

'Look in that corner,' says Linc, pointing to the back of the shop.

I see it. It's a small figure like the angel in the email. There are some other small statues and bits of marble and things. It all looks pretty grubby to me.

Then Linc casually walks into the shop. I follow but I'm a bit wary.

Inside it's quite large, like a barn, and there's a double door at the back that leads to a courtyard that looks as if it's full of similar stuff, only larger.

The shop assistants don't notice us because they are talking to some customers. Not that we are doing anything wrong. Well I'm not—yet.

'What are you looking for?' I whisper to Linc. I feel guilty but am not really sure why.

'Just looking.'

We are standing by a door that has 'PRIVATE' written on it.

Suddenly it opens. I want to bolt.

A middle-aged man steps out and gives us a quick look. 'You fellows right?' he asks gruffly as if he suspects us of something.

'Just looking,' says Linc.

'Well if you've had a good look then you can move on. I don't want young kids upsetting my customers,' he says as he makes towards a counter where a large lady is waiting. Maybe that's Winnie, I suddenly think.

'Young kids!' huffs Linc.

'I think we should go before we get caught,' I whisper.

'Get caught for what?'

'Whatever,' I say lamely. It's the only answer I can think of.

'I think we might go and have another look at those emails,' decides Linc.

We make for the door as casually as we can.

Back in the street we see the battered, red pick-up. It has a number of dirty crates on the tray, but the driver is not about.

Linc looks in the cab before we start heading off. He screws up his nose as if he has smelt something unpleasant.

When we are clear of the shop I say to Linc, 'Did you have a good look at the pick-up?'

'Sure I did.'

'See what was written on the cab near the door?'

Linc stops and looks at me suspiciously.

'What?' he demands.

I shake my head. 'You didn't notice?'

'What?' he repeats.

'Tell you later,' I yell and start running down the street, laughing.

I can hear Linc's footsteps following me but he won't catch me until we get to the ferry terminal.

When we get there we plonk down on one of the long seats and catch our breath.

'Well?' asks Linc as if the word was fired from his mouth.

I think for a second before saying, 'Couldn't have been important. I've completely forgotten!'

And I had. Just remembered it had something to do with the words on the cab.

CHAPTER 5

As soon as we get to my place I call Mama to ask if I can use the laptop. She says something which I don't catch so I get it out and open it and Linc and I have a good look at the emails.

Linc drags the graphic and the text boxes to new positions and we find the two hidden messages.

We study the first one for a while. It is a bit puzzling.

```
PosVacp48col3-4Digger
W10:8 NOGambit
```

'Where's the pens?' Linc asks.

I tell him and add that there is some paper on top of the TV.

Linc copies the message while I scratch my head.

Then we look under the angel at the second message. It is much the same gobbledegook as the first one, only a bit longer.

```
PosVacp48col3-4Digger
W10:8 NOGambit
Replyurgent
```

I can understand the last two words even if there isn't a space between them—Reply urgent. I don't explain it to Linc. He gets it too. I can tell.

Dad comes in as I am closing up the machine.

'What you fellows up to?' he says as he studies us suspiciously.

I've learnt to answer a question with a question. It can save admitting to anything. 'What's a gambit?' I ask as I put the laptop back in its place.

Dad screws up his nose and thinks before he says, 'Not real sure but I think it's something to do with … chess, or something. Something about making a move.'

Dad's not the world's greatest reader, except when it comes to a bit of music.

Mama comes in. She's been listening to us. She says, 'I don't know the real meaning, if it's got one. But I do know it's the name of one of those free newspapers you can pick up every week all over town.'

That hadn't occurred to me until Mama said it.

Dad nods approval and Linc and I exchange glances. I get the feeling we are onto something.

'That makes the N-O bit fairly easy,' says Linc.

I could even get it now. New Orleans! *The New Orleans Gambit.*

Dad and Mama are looking at us now, sorta confused.

I say excitedly, 'Where's the last one? *The Gambit,* I mean!'

'I guess it's in the bin if everyone's read it!' explains Mama. I want to tell her I hadn't read it but then I remember that I don't read it anyway. 'Bin's collected tomorrow. You might be lucky.'

I don't like the idea of ratting through our trash bin.

Charlotte just shakes her head.

Linc follows me outside. I open the lid and look in with my nose screwed up. I gingerly open the plastic liner. Linc steps right back.

'I can't see much,' I explain to Linc.

'Maybe you're not close enough,' suggests Linc with a snigger, moving even further back.

I pull open the black plastic bag a bit wider and take a quick peek inside and I straightaway feel squeamish. There's nothing near the top. I know I'm not putting my hand in the bag. I could catch the bubonic plague from the smell of it.

I push the top of the liner back into the bin and slam the lid on.

Inside, I breathe deeply.

'Wasn't there,' I tell everyone and no one in particular.

'I knew that,' says Charlotte innocently.

I stare at her with my mouth to one side.

'Took it to our activity class,' she says as if explaining the obvious.

I don't say anything. I can't see why they'd want to read a free newspaper at an activity class.

'We use it for Art,' she says, nodding her head all the while. That doesn't explain too much for me. It's been years since I was even in elementary school.

'We put it on the Art Room tables so we don't make a mess,' Charlotte shrugs.

There goes my chance for solving one of the world's greatest mysteries, I think.

CHAPTER 6

Next day Linc and I look at the text box messages again. I push Dad's mug aside. He left early to claim a position.

```
PosVacp48col3-4Digger

W10:8 NOGambit

Replyurgent
```

'We got most of the last two lines,' I mumble. '*New Orleans Gambit*, Reply urgent. But what's W10:8? Maybe it's something to do with the paper.'

Linc slaps me on the back so hard I nearly hit my head on the kitchen table.

'Well done bro!' he hoots.

I get my breath back, shake my brains back into position and stare at him blankly.

'10:8 is the date!'

Mama calls from the back room, 'You boys get a shake on. I don't want Dad upset.'

I'm not listening but trying to think what day it is. 'Today is …'

'Wednesday,' calls Charlotte who is just carrying her breakfast grits to the table.

'That's today!' beams Linc.

I agree with a nod. Then it occurs to me that I wasted my time in the smelly trash bin.

'*The Gambit* comes out today!' explains Linc, saying one word slowly at a time. I think it's so I'll understand.

'And they have a bundle of papers on the bench in the ferry terminal!' I'm with it now.

'Pick one up on the way across,' I laugh just as we hear the ferry blast as it gets near the Algiers terminal.

We grab our Nikes and rush out, yelling goodbye to Mama as we bound towards the levee.

We have minutes to spare at the terminal. People take their time getting on. The cars are a bit slower early in the morning. More of them.

I look along the seats for the paper. Someone always leaves a bundle where people can easily pick them up.

We find them by the door and both take one.

Linc, ever resourceful, has the message written on a bit of paper.

We both start flipping through the pages, hoping something will jump out at us.

I notice movement in the corner of my eye. I look up suddenly. I wish I hadn't. There, standing right in front of us, looming over us like the angels of death, are the Neville brothers. They both have silly grins on their ugly faces.

Linc hasn't noticed our company. He's still flipping through the pages. I give him a gentle elbow.

'Cut it!' he snaps.

'Linc,' I say through my teeth.

He looks up just as Eustace speaks. 'My, my. You boys can read. Bless your po' little souls.' Then, as he grabs my paper, he snarls, 'What you found that's so interesting?'

Eustace runs his eye over the page. I think he's focused on some store with the latest CDs in town.

A crowd of adults push forward and Eustace tosses the paper back at me. 'You should try the Positions Vacant.' He laughs at his weak attempt at a joke.

Lothar doesn't have much more wit. He says, as if he's just had an original thought, 'Let's move away from here. Somethin' stinks.'

I try to remember if I had a wash after ratting through our trash bin.

The ferry gives a warning blast and the attendant starts to pull the big wire gates shut.

We join the late rush for the ferry.

I make sure we are not sitting anywhere near the Neville brothers.

When the ferry pulls in at the other terminal Eustace and Lothar don't get up immediately. I think they are waiting for us.

I nudge Linc as we stand. He nods. He has noticed too. We join the far side of a group all leaving together like some slave gang.

As we pass and I'm sure we have a barrier of people between us, I call out to Eustace, in a friendly loud voice, 'How you feeling today? Useless?'

Then I start running. It doesn't take Linc long to get the message. It takes Lothar and Eustace just a mite longer but by then we have fled.

'You dumb or something?' Linc puffs, as we find Dad and saunter up as if we are really casual. 'You'll get us killed!'

Right now I don't care. I feel like I've got one up on the Neville brothers. I sit down and start putting on my Nikes. Dad's already got the tape in and running—warming the crowd up he calls it. He's playing 'Down By the Riverside'—again.

Just then I happen to look up. The Neville brothers are standing in the middle of the street looking at us.

Dad notices I've stopped tying my laces. He looks up too. He's a bit bewildered by the odd behaviour of the Neville brothers. Suddenly they make a rude gesture at us with their fingers, and storm off.

'What's the matter with those hoons?' my father asks, looking directly at me.

I shake my head, as if completely mystified. 'Must be having a bad day. Must be feeling useless,' I suggest, as I start working on my laces again.

Dad gives up at this stage but Linc elbows me in the ribs, 'Useless is better than brain dead like someone I know!'

'Maybe you should try the Positions Vacant too,' I mutter. His attitude is spoiling my fun.

Suddenly Linc stops fiddling with his shoes. I can sense it.

I look at him. I can almost see the light bulb popping out of his head. It's shining nearly as brightly as the smile on his face. Talk about mood changes!

'What's up now?' I question.

'Tell you later,' he smirks.

'Wow!' I say to myself. 'I can't wait.'

CHAPTER 7

On our afternoon return to the terminal we make sure the Neville brothers aren't lurking in some doorway waiting to pounce.

When the ferry comes we get seats on the top deck and watch the late arrivals. No Nevilles. The metal gates clang shut and the ferry gives a hoot and pulls out into the middle of the river.

'Okay, give!' I say.

'You didn't tell me about the red pick-up,' Linc accuses.

He's right but I've totally forgotten. All I can do is shrug and say, 'Forgotten.'

'Couldn't have been important,' he says as he opens his paper. He goes to a back section. I wait patiently, pretending to look at the Algiers terminal.

'Got it,' he says proudly.

'Well, I haven't,' I grumble.

'PosVac! Positions Vacant! They've put something in the Positions Vacant columns!'

I didn't know there was such a thing in *The Gambit*.

Linc takes the bit of paper from his pocket. It's looking pretty limp by now. 'p – 48,' he mumbles.

In a burst of inspiration I say, 'Page 48!' But I say it in a dissatisfied mumble.

'Good,' agrees Linc. Then he goes on, 'It's all here—so obvious! Column three—for Digger.'

'Who's Digger?'

'Digger is the person wanted in the ad.' Linc's finger jabs the ad in column three.

I can't remain aloof any longer. I unfold my rolled paper and find the ad. It is certainly an ad for someone wanting a digger. It's not at all clear to me if it's a person they want or a digging machine.

★ DIGGER REQUIRED ★

Casual night work for four men
10:10/17/24?9pm
No transport required
Part-time garden work at Underhill and Co.

'It doesn't make much sense,' I observe. 'There's no address. Or phone number.'

Linc says, 'Probably like the email. It's a secret message. They don't want people to know what they are up to.'

'We could look Underhill up in the phone book,' I suggest.

Linc agrees but thinks it's a long shot. Underhill could also be a place.

I can't think of anybody or any place called Underhill, or even Underwood. Anyway, why would they want diggers and gardeners at night?

The ferry gives a warning hoot. We are almost across the river. We stand and head for the rail to watch her dock.

Suddenly I say, 'I remember what was on the truck!'

But Linc's not listening. 'Step back!' he hisses as he lowers his body.

I follow suit but I look inquiringly at him. The other passengers must have thought we were nuts!

'The Neville boys are on the terminal waiting for the ferry to come in,' Linc says through tight lips.

We are back a fair way and stand cautiously. We can still see the tops of their heads but they haven't seen us.

'Where are they going?' I ask. I'm not sure I expected an answer.

'In my humble opinion, they're not going anywhere. They are waiting to meet *someone* leaving the ferry.'

I almost breathe a sigh of relief, then it hits me. They are waiting for us!

'We could try and make a run for it,' suggests Linc. 'Move off with the crowd.'

I have a better idea. 'Let's pretend we are not on the ferry. We go across and back again.'

Linc nods approval. We hide on the far side of the ferry's upper deck where we can see the Neville brothers but they can't see us.

There is still the chance that they could come aboard and check the ferry out. Linc thinks that unlikely. There are too many places to hide and it might also give us a chance to make a break for it.

Eustace looks at his watch. The last passengers have disembarked and the new passengers are boarding.

Lothar says something angrily to his big brother. They are not in a happy mood.

Finally the ferry pulls away from the jetty. I'm tempted to go up to the rail and wave to the Nevilles, but for once common sense prevails—just.

Luckily for me because they are still at the terminal when we return.

We do three return trips before it seems safe to get off. I think the crew are getting a bit suspicious by that time.

Trouble is it is now dark.

We decide to go home down the streets rather than over the levee. They'd expect us to use the levee path if they are still intent on doing us some harm.

We don't exactly run home but we keep up a good pace. Try to look like young joggers.

'By the way,' Linc puffs in front of me, 'what was on the red pick-up?'

But I'm too exhausted to go into deep discussion. 'Tell you later,' I pant.

'Uh-huh,' pants Linc but I don't think he believes me.

CHAPTER 8

Linc goes straight home but the minute I get inside the house and catch my breath, I start to study the ad. If it is a secret message I am going to crack it.

Mama makes some wisecrack about working late but I ignore it.

I spread the paper out on the table and start to puzzle over the ad.

Mama sees me poring over the paper. 'Can't be school work,' she comments. She looks over my shoulder and I tap the ad I'm reading.

'Why are you looking for a job?' she asks, a bit puzzled.

I explain as briefly as I can that I think it's a phoney ad.

'Sure don't seem real smart. There's no phone number or address or anything,' she says, looking more closely at the ad.

★ DIGGER REQUIRED ★
Casual night work for four men
10:10/17/24?9pm
No transport required
Part-time garden work at Underhill and Co.

I tell her I had already noticed that. Then she becomes serious. 'Who's this Underhill? I've never heard of any Underhills here.'

That answers one of my questions but I don't say so.

Just then Dad comes in with two plastic bags of groceries from a small store just down the road.

He looks at us studying *The Gambit* and Mama tries to explain. Then I try to explain, which seems to confuse him all the more.

'You know any Underhills?' Mama asks.

Dad thinks for a while and I nearly get bored waiting, then he shakes his head.

He joins Mama in looking over my shoulder. 'Got that bit,' he says, pointing at the second line. 'Something's happening at nine o'clock. Maybe that's the time for the job interview. Nine o'clock in the morning is about the right time for a job interview to start.'

'Dad, it's nine p.m.! But it sounds right,' I agree.

'It's a bit of a mystery. Wouldn't want to go for a job at nine at night!' Dad agrees.

'Well, if that's the time then those numbers are the dates!' Mama decides.

And she is right. It's all so obvious—when you know. October 10, 17 and 24. All a week apart.

'Three lots of interviews,' says Mama. 'They must expect lots of applicants.'

Dad and I both explain that it's not a real ad. It's a secret message for someone. I haven't said anything about the emails and Mr Moore.

Dad says, 'I reckon the question mark means that day—or the night—of the 24th is still to be finalised.'

And, I think, sometimes parents aren't all that dumb. It's obvious—when you know!

'The first date's only two days away. That don't give much warning for interviews—or anything,' says Mama.

I reconsider my original opinion about parents *not* being dumb.

I don't say anything about the emails but I think that maybe time is getting short for whoever is going to be doing whatever, wherever—and whenever.

It's then I realise I haven't really solved much at all!

'Too puzzling for me,' Mama finally decides and leaves with a parting comment. 'Underhill! Sounds like Underground. Maybe it's a railway.'

I ignore the last part of her comment but I see a connection. Digger and Underhill! My heart's starting to race like the beginning of a drum roll. I have a feeling I'm onto something.

Dad gives a shrug and switches on the TV. He likes to watch TV while he helps Mama get food prepared, except that it takes most of his concentration.

If I had enough money I'd buy him a new one.

I look at the ad again. A digger for some underground or underhill work. Who digs, I wonder. And why four men and why at night?

I start thinking about road diggers, ditch diggers, gold diggers, grave diggers. We don't have to dig graves in New Orleans. People are buried above the ground in tombs. But there's something about the idea that intrigues me. It could be a sneaky way of saying something about cemeteries.

The more I think about it the more I like the idea. It feels right. I wonder if it's a secret message for people who are into voodoo and black magic. Makes sense. Sure is enough of them in New Orleans, although I sometimes wonder if it's not just a bit of hoo-hah put on for the tourists.

'No transport required' would fit in too. The organisers would have their own transport vehicles for people wanting to go to the cemetery for a bit of a voodoo thrill. Like my dad says, some fools and their money are easily parted.

Time would be right too!

But then I read the ad again. There are too many bits that don't fit in—yet. Surely they wouldn't be into sacrifices and things. A chilling thought. I give a shudder. I'm starting to get gruesome.

All the same, I reckon I'm onto something.

Suddenly at my elbow is a plate of chicken pieces, done Cajun style. The ad can wait.

I pick up the plate and head for the rocker on the front verandah. Dad won't want it. He'll be real busy watching TV and eating.

Sitting on the verandah I get stuck into the chicken. I hadn't realised how hungry I had got. So much happening, not to mention three rides across the river, all the time wondering what the Neville boys were up to.

I look across the street to the shrubbery of the opposite houses. It looks quite dark away from the streetlights. A riverboat gives a lonesome blast of its whistle, which startles me a bit, even though I must have heard it a thousand times.

Suddenly I think I see movement in the shadows across the street. My heart misses a beat. I'm being watched, I'm sure, although I can't see anything. But I can feel it.

I stare at the shadows unblinkingly until my eyes ache. By that time everything is starting to swim in the darkness.

Then I hear a noise like a twig breaking. I'm getting really nervous but trying to look calm.

I stand up, holding my plate, and walk to the edge of the verandah.

All is silent. Strangely too silent.

I walk down to the front gate and look up and down the street. I still feel safe—but afraid.

I look back to the dark shrubbery. Then I see something move. A leafy branch seems to fly back into place. It's as if it was being held down, or aside, and was suddenly let go to flick back into place.

I know branches don't do that by themselves. I want to call out, but that would be inviting trouble. So I just stand at the gate with my empty plate in my hand.

After a minute or so I decide to go back inside. As I do I hear footsteps racing down the darkened street. I look and can make out two shadows heading for the levee path. I hear the shadows grunting up the bank and then for a brief moment I see them silhouetted against the city lights as they slip past a gap between the roofs of two houses.

The shadows have about the same size and shape as the Neville brothers.

For some mad reason I suddenly remember what was on the red pick-up.

I hurry inside and on top of *The Gambit* page I write 'Winston Samuels Property Renovations and Excavations'. That way I won't forget it—again. I'm not really sure it's important but it is a bit more info about Peter Moore.

Then I just wait for a few minutes getting my composure. There are connections somewhere between all the bits of the puzzle but I don't see them.

CHAPTER 9

Next day Dad and I arrive in Royal Street before Linc. Sometimes he just sleeps in. Dad said we couldn't wait for him. I have a nervous feeling about Linc after last night and the ferry incident. I hope nothing serious has happened to him.

I keep glancing down the street hoping to see him coming.

Dad notices. 'You still worried about the Nevilles?'

'Naw,' I say with an offhand shrug.

Dad starts playing 'The Saints' to warm up the crowd—not that it is a big one. Two guys with banjos, just down the street, are doing some blue grass impersonations. I could sense Dad thinking that they are interfering with his music.

At least they are attracting a bit of an audience.

And just for a moment I forget about Linc and he turns up.

'How are you today Linc?' queries Dad. 'You okay?'

'Sure,' says Linc, although I can tell he's not too sure why Dad is questioning him.

I catch Linc's eye and tap my copy of *The Gambit*. Linc gets my message.

At lunchtime we manage to get a bit of a break. Dad wants to see a fellow about some old records he's got stashed away. Linc and I head for Jackson Square and find a bench where we can talk.

Along the fence is a whole bunch of paintings on old French Quarter slate. Most of them are of jazz players in some sort of archway with the moonlight or streetlights behind them. Supposed to be romantic—or something.

'Tell you what I've worked out,' I say to Linc. I don't say anything about the help my parents gave me.

I explain to Linc about the dates. Linc reckons he got that much. Then I tell him about my cemetery ideas. It doesn't sound so good in broad daylight, but to my surprise Linc is interested.

'I bet there's a connection!' he says, punching his palm. He opens the paper to the ad. I do the same. I think we must look like a couple of old men reading our free papers in the sunshine.

'Let's assume it's got something to do with the cemetery,' says Linc, 'and see what fits in.'

I look at the ad and suggest, 'Maybe the transport is to carry the bodies?'

Linc doesn't even bother to reply. It's a bit lame.

I decide there and then not to say anything about seeing the Neville brothers the night before. It's not so scary now. And, I tell myself, I can't really be sure it was them anyway. Light can play funny tricks.

'We could test the idea,' he says slowly. 'Let's go up to St Louis No. 1 Cemetery tomorrow night at nine o'clock!'

St Louis Cemetery is up past Rampart Street. It's general knowledge you don't go up there at night unless you want to die—of fright or mortal wounds—take your pick!

I'm not game to say no.

'Tell you what,' says Linc. And he does. He wants to go up to Rampart Street now and find a suitable, safe place to watch the approach to the cemetery then go back tomorrow night, before it's too dark and just see who goes in.

I think about who might—or might not—come out.

But Linc's all fired up and I follow him up Bourbon Street towards Conti Street.

We have forgotten all about the Neville brothers doing their thing in Bourbon Street. Suddenly we are opposite them. They have a small crowd of amused watchers. I think they're amused because the Neville brothers' dancing is pretty heavy-footed.

They aren't getting much money. Lothar has a scowl that is thinly hidden behind a forced smile.

We stop to watch—sus out the competition, if you like. After all we are pretty safe. There are lots of people in the street. I can't see the Nevilles breaking their routine just to give me a thumping.

The music stops and Mr Lenny Neville goes around with the tip-tin. I reckon people put money in because they feel hassled, but some tourists are all smiles about our quaint little Nawlin ways.

The Neville boys sidle slowly through the crowd towards us.

'What you want?' says Eustace. It sounds more like a threat than a genuine inquiry.

I say, before I can stop myself, 'Seeing if I can see a thick *loaf a'* bread.' The minute I say it I know it's a mistake. It wasn't even clever. In fact, it was stupid!

Lothar looks at his big brother for some sort of signal.

Linc grabs my elbow and steers me roughly through the thin crowd like I'm under arrest. 'You got some sort of death wish?' he hisses.

The Neville boys don't follow us, except with their eyes. As we turn into Conti Street I have a quick look back. I can see Eustace watching us as we leave. Not a good sign!

Linc doesn't say too much until we cross Rampart Street and can see the cemetery. It's a bit of a shock for me. It's not at all spooky. It's all clean and whitewashed and neat. Doesn't look like voodoo territory at all.

We walk right up to the entrance. I see the crypts and vaults. Some, with their little peaked roofs, look like miniature buildings. Many have little fences around them made from wrought iron. The uprights look like black spears.

It's like a little town—except all the inhabitants are dead. A town of the dead!

In the cemetery the haphazard arrangement of the crypts certainly provides a variety of hiding places where we could wait and observe but they would also obscure any dangers to us. Hiding in the cemetery doesn't appeal to either of us.

Nearby there's a deserted, derelict cottage. We pick out a couple of spots where we could hide and watch the entrance without too much fear of being discovered.

I unwrap my paper, which by now is pretty grotty, and re-read the ad.

Linc looks over my arm.

'What's that?' he asks, pointing to the words I have written.

'Winston Samuel's Property Renovations and Excavations. The name on the red pick-up,' I explain. 'I wrote it there so I wouldn't forget it.'

'Interesting,' says Linc. 'Tell you later,' he smirks.

'Wow!' I say to myself. 'I can't wait.'

I'm about to object but he has already turned and is waiting at the kerb for the traffic to clear on Rampart Street. Duty calls.

I do a quick about turn and follow. I also have a good look around the place. I'm starting to expect a Neville brother in every shadow or behind every parked car.

And I see movement near an old boarding house. It was almost too quick but I'm sure I saw something. Nothing definite but it sure looked like someone ducking for cover. Someone about the size of Useless Eustace!

'Linc!' I call towards the street.

I was too occupied to see the next slight movement disappearing behind the corner of the boarding house.

'Linc!' I call again, only a bit louder.

CHAPTER 10

inc turns and looks at me as if he's bewildered.

I make some funny hand signals, trying to point to the boarding house without being obvious. No doubt it *is* a fairly obvious thing to do. Linc peers at the boarding house with furrows in his brow. Then he looks back at me.

I shake my head while holding my body stiff.

Linc's getting really confused. He does an open-handed shrug and returns to where I am standing.

I tell him what I think I saw. He doesn't really believe me.

I do a furtive survey of the whole area. Three hundred and sixty degrees of it—or is that three hundred and eighty?

All I see is a small crowd of tourists crossing Rampart Street behind a tour leader. They are about to start a cemetery tour. Some people will hand over cash for anything!

Linc sees the tour group too, which gives him an idea.

Linc explains that if we tag along with the group we'll be able to watch without being obvious. It seems like a good idea to me until I see that everyone in the group is wearing a little round sticker on their clothes that reads: 'French Quarter and Cemetery Tour'.

I point this out to Linc with a quick flick of my wrist.

Linc shrugs. I swear it's becoming a habit!

We follow the crowd into the cemetery.

The tour leader huddles the group together near some family tombs and vaults. Some of the group find some shade near the larger crypts. The first thing the leader does is explain how unsafe the cemeteries are for visitors and unwary tourists.

At this point Linc rubs his chin like some old man having a bit of a think.

The leader goes on to explain that the local Tourist Association is providing a reward for information about anyone damaging the crypts, tombs and vaults. I think he's warning anyone who is thinking about souveniring a piece of cemetery.

'Don't even scratch a cross in the paintwork,' he finishes smugly.

'The crypts might not be the home of vampires and ghosts,' he explains, as if he knows what he's saying off by heart, 'but they are often the haunts of more dangerous types. I know of some police officers who won't come in to some of the cemeteries at night unless they are wearing protective clothing and have at least four other officers with them.'

'Should get some real coppers,' jokes a heckler in the group. He has an odd accent.

There's a nervous giggle from some of the tour group.

'You'd better believe it. If you are in here at night and you start screaming, no one, but no one, will come running to help you. And if you think you can put out a mayday on your cell phone—forget it. The derros or the junkies or the muggers will already have your phone! You remember the film *Easy Rider*? That was made here. They don't admit it but the locals know it was based upon facts.'

He looks around with a self-satisfied smile.

He then goes on to explain why all the tombs and vaults are above ground. Something to do with floods and mud.

Then he spots Linc and me.

I'm all for running but Linc stands his ground as casually as you like.

'You kids right?' the leader asks, meaning are you part of this group? Have you paid? If not, then clear off.

'Thought it safer to stay with a group,' I mumble loudly. I wanted to say, 'and we ain't kids!'

Someone in the group gives me a little appreciative clap. I feel embarrassed. The group leader decides not to risk losing face so he merely ignores us and continues his spiel. 'Some of the dead are placed in these vaults.' He points to a bank of openings that look like whitewashed school lockers, only deeper.

He continues, 'They slide the coffins in there and seal it up. A year and a day later they can open it and what do you think remains?'

There are a few wild guesses.

'Practically nothing except a few old bones and a few bits of wood. Lot of ash. The whole lot has effectively been cremated by the hot Louisiana sun! Ashes to ashes, dust to dust in a year and a day.' Another self-satisfied smile.

'What about if it's a leap year, mate?' calls the heckler. I think he's an Australian.

I'm starting to think this is not the place to be at night—without protection. Maybe we should buy a cross—or some garlic.

Suddenly Linc jabs me in the ribs. I'm so startled that I give a little gasp, which gets a smart comment from the tour leader who then goes on to explain who has been 'buried' there and how the family crypts work. Louis the vampire even has a tomb here—empty. He lets us wonder about that!

'The famous voodoo queen Marie Laveau has her final resting place just over there,' the tour guide points at a tomb. 'You may place tokens, Mardi Gras beads or change at it. Some people even place a lighted candle there and ask her favours.'

This is pretty weird stuff, I think, when Linc hisses in my ear, 'You were right. Just saw Eustace hurrying across the road.'

Not good news.

'Think we should get back. Yer Dad'll be getting worried,' says Linc, looking at his watch.

As we turn to leave, the leader has one passing shot, 'Hope you enjoyed the free lecture boys!'

I turn and say, 'I was waiting for the bit about the mad dog that breaks open the vaults to eat the pre-cooked human remains!'

There are a few funny noises from the group. Someone calls out to the leader, 'Hey, tell us about that one, mate.' Has to be an Australian.

I'm glad to escape the tour leader's lecture but I manage to convince Linc not to go back the way we came.

Linc taps me on the shoulder, 'How'd you know about the mad dog?'

I reply, 'Didn't. Made it up.'

Linc just says, 'Motormouth!' I don't think it was praise.

But underneath my cool exterior I'm starting to get jittery. I don't know if it's the prospect of cemeteries at night or the Neville brothers waylaying us in some narrow, lonely alley.

Dad's not happy with us being late. But that's just part of the game. As soon as he sees us he has the tape recorder running. It's 'Sweet Georgia Brown'. At least it's a change from 'The Saints'!

CHAPTER 11

After we finish performing for the day Linc suggests that I go over to his place for a while. He wants to show me something on his computer.

We have an incident-free ferry trip but we are on high alert all the time. Heads swinging this way and that. We are both a bit nervy.

I give Mama a call from the street just to let her know what I'm doing. Charlotte wants to come over too but before she can get an answer from Mama we have hung up and hightailed it down the street.

Linc lives next to a small convenience store that has the craziest hours. I have to stop and read the sign each time I pass the place.

> ## STORE HOURS
>
> Open most days about 9 or 10, occasionally as early as 7, but some days as late as 12 or 1. We close about 5:30 or 6, occasionally about 4 or 5, but sometimes as late as 11 or 12. Some days or afternoons we aren't here at all but lately I've been here just about all the time except when I'm some place else.
>
> — Billy G

I'm about to ask if Billy G really owns the store but Linc grabs me by the elbow and hauls me off to his place.

Linc boots up the family computer while I say hello to his parents.

'Look at this Xav,' Linc calls.

I look over his shoulder at the screen. He has opened up the email program. He asks, 'What's the first thing you do when you want to send an email?'

I answer, 'I usually put the address of the person I'm emailing.'

'Right. But most machines you don't have to put the full address. You start keying and the machine finishes it for you if it's in your address book. Your contacts. It has them in alphabetical order.'

I go, 'Uh-huh,' but I'm not really sure what Linc's on about.

'Now just suppose I want to send an email to Carson. I start typing C-A-R and bingo the machine has done the rest!' says Linc as he sits back with a big smile.

I look at the address line but there's something not right. 'But it says Carnegie, not Carson! The machine made a mistake.'

'Not really,' explains Linc, 'If I had keyed the next letter—S—then the machine would have written Carson. What people often fail to do is to check closely that the machine has put in the right address. It's pre-emptive!'

'Pre-emptied?' I say with a scowl.

'Emptived!' says Linc as if I have a hearing problem. 'Now to your problem—Samson.'

'I do have a first name,' I say in no uncertain terms.

But Linc ignores me and goes on to explain that probably what happened was that Peter Moore went to type in someone else's name but our name came up.

I can't think whose name Peter Moore would be sending an email to and say so.

'Xavier, think for a moment. You wrote it in your paper!' There's an element of exasperation in Linc's tone.

'Samuels?'

'Samuels,' agrees Linc. 'Peter Moore started keying S-A-M and he expected the computer to complete the name Samuels. Instead it completed the name Samson.'

I nod slowly but then I think of something. 'Why would Peter Moore have our email address?' I think it's a good question.

'Probably got it from someone who was doing a bulk emailing. Had plenty of cc addresses. You'd be surprised how many business people have you on their machines. People who don't even know you.'

I accept that, then say slowly, 'So it looks like Samuels and Moore have something funny going on if they are sending secret messages. And the ad said something about wanting a digger.' Then it hits me. 'Excavators are diggers! He does excavation work. It was on his pick-up.'

'I reckon it's more than funny—I reckon it's gotta be criminal!'

I think about the ad. We seem to be breaking the code but there are still some bits that need explaining. Bits that don't make sense—yet. We really don't have any idea what they might be doing wrong. Just a lot of suspicions.

'Do you reckon they are graverobbers? Winston Samuels and his gang?' I suddenly ask Linc. The idea had just occurred to me. 'Used to be a lot of that in the old days. Seen it in films.'

'What did you say?' Linc is looking at me as if he'd missed an important point.

I start to say about the graverobbers but he shakes his head.

'What would you call Winston?' he asks.

I've lost the thread of his reasoning somewhere. I offer, 'A crook? A thief?'

'I mean *Winston*? What would you call Winston if you were real friendly like?'

I know it's not Mr Samuels so I say, 'Win?' Sounds silly.

'Winnie?' says Linc, rolling his eyes.

The name in the emails. Winnie is a man not a woman!

We are silent for a moment or two just nodding our heads. It's all so obvious—when you know. Twenty-twenty vision—in hindsight!

But Linc still hasn't answered my earlier question. I repeat it. 'Are they graverobbers?'

Linc thinks for a moment, then gives a shrug. 'With a bit of luck we'll know a lot more tomorrow night.'

I had pushed the thought of the cemetery visit right out of my mind. It was suddenly getting too close. I had visions of the dead escaping from their burial chambers as Moore and Samuels opened them to steal jewellery and anything else of value. I was starting to get a bit apprehensive.

Two dolts wandering around a cemetery at night would be easy pickings for the undead. Needless to say I didn't dawdle on my way back home.

CHAPTER 12

The next day Dad has things to do rather than badger us to tap-dance in the Quarter. I think he gives music lessons to some kids out around Gretna Way. Then he gets with some of his old buddies and they jam for a while, like in the good ol' days—last century!

That afternoon late Linc and I dream up an excuse to go back across the river. It was a pretty lame excuse but our mothers are tired of trying to keep tabs on us. My dad says boys have gotta be men sooner or later and the sooner the better. I'm not real sure what he means.

I take a pen light and Linc has a larger torch. He looks at my pen light with contempt.

We make our way up to the ferry terminal just a few minutes after the ferry has pulled in. A couple of vehicles come off and a few drive on. Parking is in a confined space on the lower deck. Engines turned off.

No sign of the Neville brothers—so far. We board the ferry, go upstairs and watch the last of the passengers come aboard. The coast seems clear.

The ferry casts off into the midstream current and we relax for a few minutes. But I'm restless and a bit nervous. The idea of hanging around a cemetery at night, even if it is St Louis No. 1 doesn't fill me full of courage.

I wander around to the other side of the stairwell. I'm not expecting anything to happen, not until I see the Neville brothers sitting there grinning at me. It's like I've walked into the Brer Fox and Brer Rabbit tar-baby trap. My heart misses about thirty beats before I turn and run. The Neville boys just take their time, stand and head in the direction I'm going.

I yell at Linc to move out. 'The Nevilles!' Some passengers eye us with disapproval. Linc follows me but there aren't too many places to go.

We head downstairs to the vehicle deck—three steps at a time.

Not many spots to hide down here either! I thought the place would be loaded with hiding places.

'Gotta try and keep out of their reach until we hit the other side,' Linc gasps. He looks around madly for somewhere to go. I check the stairs and I can see four feet coming down, nice and slowly.

'Toilets!' I say.

Linc shakes his head. 'Be trapped in there. You can bet your skinny hide no one would come in to help us.'

We move away from the stairs, past a couple of cars and towards a small truck with a canopy-covered tray. I'm so scared I can't think but Linc is an opportunist. He pushes aside the back flaps, climbs into the back of the truck and hisses for me to follow. I skin my ankle getting in but we are soon under cover. It's like being in a tent.

Then we just sit there, in the dim light, on some half-full bags of corn or something equally as hard. Maybe it's potatoes. The bags smell as if they are full of dirt.

I hardly dare to breathe but we listen until our ears hurt. Then we hear them walk up and stand beside the truck for a few moments.

Lothar swears like he has just learned to do it.

'Bet they're in the toilet,' says Eustace smugly. 'Wait here.'

Doesn't have to wait long. The toilet door slams and Eustace decides to have a bit of a swear. 'Well, they didn't jump ship halfway 'cross!' he finally concludes. 'Look for feet under the cars. Could be hiding behind one of the cars.'

We hear Lothar grunt as he gets down low to look beneath the cars. 'Can't see nothing,' he says.

Just then the ferry gives a blast. We are just about on the other side. Drivers return. Car doors are closed and a couple of the less patient drivers start their engines as the ferry swings in the current trying to line up with the exit ramp.

The truck rocks as the driver climbs on board, yanks his door shut and starts his engine as the ferry settles into a fixed position. Metal gates clang into place and gas fumes seem to be thick enough to choke us, then we are up the ramp and away.

We are trapped on the truck. No idea where we could end up—maybe North Dakota! Or Mexico!

We hit the major railway crossing fairly fast and I bounce back and hit my head on the back of the cab. I let out a yelp. Then the bag of whatever rolls over and hits the floor. Another cry of pain.

The truck bounces across the next track and this time my head hits the steel frame supporting the canvas canopy. It's like being in a torture chamber. I curse loudly.

Linc grits his teeth.

The truck slams to a sudden stop and before we can get out, the driver's door opens, then slams shut. The back flaps of the canopy are yanked apart and a big black man peers at us with a menacing look.

'Get out!' he demands. I don't think we have much choice. 'What the hell are you doing in there? Bloody thieves!'

As we scramble over the tailgate I try to explain. I don't make much sense.

'Saw your buddies too. What do they do? Cause the distraction while you two hoods lift stuff from innocent people!'

'Not our buddies,' I retort a bit louder than I expected.

'Tell it to the judge.'

By this time we are down on the ground but he is barring any possible quick escape. He's a big man and he seems as mad as an angry rattlesnake.

'Names!' he demands. I see that his fist is clenched.

'Names?' both Linc and I say as if we don't understand the question.

'Yeah, names! You act like thieves you get treated like thieves. I got a brother that's a cop! Names!'

I say, 'Lothar.'

I think I can sense Linc's horror.

'Lothar who?'

'Lothar Neville. And this is my big brother, Eustace. Eustace Neville.'

Linc's pretty wide-eyed by now.

The man repeats the names so that he won't forget them. 'Not names I'm likely to forget in a hurry. Now get away from my truck.'

We shuffle sideways, keeping as far from those big fists as possible.

'Get!' he yells and we run.

In a moment we hear the truck roar off, then we sit down on the kerb.

Linc looks at me. 'You're mad. What if the Neville brothers find out you have dobbed them in for something they didn't do. They'll kill us!'

I hadn't thought that far ahead. I give a helpless shrug.

'Motormouth!' says Linc with a sigh of despair.

A train whistles mournfully somewhere down the river. Matches my feelings.

CHAPTER 13

When we reach Rampart Street we hang back for a while before crossing, sticking to the side streets and the cover of vehicles and rusty, battered dumpsters that seemed to be filled to overflowing with anything from waste building material to black bags of household garbage.

As the sun sets and twilight falls we are getting a bit jittery. Linc is trying not to look it but I can tell he's nervy.

I think I'd jump right out of my skin if someone unexpectedly said 'Boo!'

'Been thinking about the Neville brothers,' he says thoughtfully.

'Yeah?' I say, not trying to encourage any more criticism of my lies to the truck driver.

'Do you reckon they are tied up in this whole business?'

That takes me by surprise. I look at Linc just as the streetlights come on.

Linc explains, 'I reckon they might know we are onto them.'

'Who?'

'Well, remember when you returned that email. It would have had your email address on it. Moore and Samuels probably worked it out from that.'

I get a sinking feeling in my stomach. 'But why the Nevilles?'

'My guess is that they have been called in to scare us off.'

'It's working,' I confirm.

'Think about it. They always seem to be around when we start digging into this mystery.'

I wish he hadn't used the word 'digging'. I'm really getting the jitters. I look across the street towards St Louis No. 1.

Linc continues, 'You know their dad's got a bit of a record—and both the brothers have been in a bit of strife.'

My dad had told us about some of the things ol' man Neville had got up to but I hadn't heard about any recent stuff.

Linc next suggests that it may be time to cross the road to have a better view of the cemetery gate. His plan is that we go across separately so that we don't look like a pair.

He goes first, dashing across between a stream of traffic. I have to wait for five minutes just to see if Linc is followed.

Linc makes it safely across and heads towards a parked truck for cover.

It's getting darker, shadowier.

The smell from the dumpster I'm hiding behind is making me feel sick. I'm sure there's a dead body in it. Maybe a corpse that graverobbers took from the cemetery.

I flick my pen light on and check my watch.

Three minutes have gone. Two to go.

I look over my shoulder and peer into the shadows to where people could be hiding. I can't see any movement but if they are in the shadows and not moving then obviously I am hardly likely to. It's too quiet.

The quiet before the storm—or hurricane. Dad says the last one, Hurricane Alicia, was a wild one when it hit.

A light breeze sneaks across the street and gives me a full whiff of what I'm crouching next to. It's not nice.

I look at my watch again. Four and a half minutes gone. That's close enough for me. With a quick glance back down the side street and another along Rampart Street, I'm off.

In my hurry I don't take too much notice of the traffic flow. A few angry blasts of horns has me ducking and tumbling for safety onto the grassy neutral territory in the middle of the road.

I lie on the grass for a moment before looking up. I can see the silhouette of Linc's head and shoulders around the nose of the truck. I can tell he's concerned but I manage a wave to dismiss his fears.

I'm a little more circumspect in crossing the second half of the road.

Behind the truck Linc pretends deep concern now that I'm safe. 'You were supposed to do it without attracting attention. I think everyone for ten miles around must be wondering what that commotion was! You certainly know how to get people looking!'

I dust my sleeves and refuse to answer. I'm not even going to apologise.

Linc breathes in through his nose then lets out a deep sigh. He moves off, beckoning me to follow like some lowly slave.

Linc wants to check out the deserted house across the street and down by the cemetery before it gets too dark. Maybe there are squatters in it, he reasons.

But it seems deserted. No lights, no sound. A weary FOR SALE sign is leaning towards the cemetery gate as if it's about to lie down and die. The front fence hardly exists. And there are a few untrimmed shrubs behind the fence that is remaining.

We make our way warily towards the shrubbery. It has thick foliage and enough room to make a reasonably comfortable hiding place.

We settle into our positions and begin the wait. Who will the diggers be, I wonder.

'Keep an eye out for four men,' advises Linc. 'Wish I had a po' boy.'

Food is the last thing on my mind. The very thought of it nearly makes me retch. The smell from the dumpster has soaked into my clothes—and my skin.

Watching is easy at first. There are hardly any pedestrians on the streets. The cars are whizzing through.

'Look!' Linc suddenly hisses.

There are two shadowy characters lurking on the far side of Rampart Street, waiting for a break in the traffic.

'Only two,' I whisper, even though they must be a hundred yards away.

'Give the rest time,' advises Linc.

We watch the pair slink across the street and then up towards the lane to the cemetery.

'Maybe it's not them,' says Linc after a few moments.

But I have a clearer view than Linc. I jab him gently in the ribs. 'It's them alright. It's the Neville brothers.'

That shocks Linc. And I'm thinking that maybe Linc's theory about the Neville brothers being part of the whole mystery could just be right. They have come to sort us out, scare us off.

The brothers reach the laneway and have a good look up and down the street and towards the gate of the cemetery. They must be looking right over our heads. It suddenly seems a lot brighter than it was twenty minutes ago.

I hunch my shoulders trying to make myself as small as possible.

The Neville brothers move stealthily down the street and then stop just beyond the fence where we are hiding.

They are talking in loud whispers but I'm shaking too much to hear what they are saying.

I hope they aren't looking for a hiding place as well. This one is so obvious.

One of the pair flicks a torch on and flashes it up and down the road. I hold my breath until it goes off.

Meanwhile, Eustace does a complete, but slow, three-sixty-degree sweep of the area with his eyes.

My palms become clammy and it's not just the Nawlins' humidity.

For a moment I swear his eyes linger on the shrubs where we are barely concealed.

CHAPTER 14

Eustace growls, 'Let's move along.'

To my relief the Neville brothers move up towards the cemetery gate. We both slowly rise to a semi-squatting position, just keeping lower than the top spindly branches of the shrub that is our cover.

'Gone in!' declares Linc as he stands with hunched shoulders.

I'm not sure what our plan of action is now but I think we should wait and see if another two 'diggers' turn up. Then we could head for home. I'm not for getting tangled with four felons bigger than me. At least we now know we are somehow on the right track.

Linc is still standing, watching, waiting.

I'm all for keeping low so I'm back on the ground under the shrub.

A siren wails in the distance. It's getting closer. A sudden fear makes me shudder. What if the police have been tipped off that we are in the area and are expected to commit some grisly crime?

The siren gets louder.

Suddenly Linc steps out from behind the shrub and fence and back into the lane. 'Coming?' he calls softly.

'Home?' hopefully I mutter.

The siren roars past along Rampart Street. It's not us they are after.

'Don't be a moron. To the cemetery,' he whispers in exasperation, completely ignoring the police siren.

Remembering the comment about derros, junkies and muggers all I can make is a feeble little groan, and rub my sweating hands down my jeans.

Without looking back Linc begins to edge his way towards the gate, hugging the boundary line of the old houses. With little choice I hurry to catch up, almost barging into him when he suddenly stops.

I'm sure he glared at me but it's getting too difficult to see clearly.

We reach the gate and stop and wait, peering into the darkness. The crypts are a bundle of overlapping silhouettes against the dim night lights of suburban New Orleans. Not a reassuring sight.

We stand motionless for what seems like ages.

Then suddenly we see it. The flash of a torch beam on some distant crypts. It lasts just a few brief seconds.

'There,' I hiss, pointing.

'See it,' replies Linc. 'Somewhere over the other side.'

We wait again.

Another flash.

'Near the middle!' I hiss, heart beating loud enough to wake the dead. 'Getting closer.'

'Still just two of them, as far as I can gather,' Linc says. 'Let's go.'

Those words are real jazz to my aching ears, until I realise he means into the cemetery. I want to explain how dangerous it is but my teeth have started chattering.

Glumly I follow Linc past the vaults and into the cemetery proper.

Another flash.

Like a pair of dancers, in unison we bob down low next to each other. The beam flashes above our heads on the top of some of the crypts. The Neville brothers are still several cemetery lanes away.

Tapping my shoulder Linc says, without looking at me, 'We can wait here and see what they are up to.'

We wait in a crouched position. The torch beam flashes move away, then back again as if they are combing the lanes.

'Don't have much of a plan,' Linc observes, referring to the Neville brothers. 'More like tourists than thieves.'

They are quite close now and they are working their way between some haphazardly aligned crypts.

My thighs are starting to ache. I think, I can't run if I've got cramps in both legs.

I hold my breath and Linc squats motionlessly.

'Haven't been along this one,' I hear one of the brothers say. Reckon it was Lothar.

A beam of light flashes along the ground just behind my shoes. I tap Linc on the shoulder.

The beam sweeps up and down the path behind my feet again. Edging closer.

It's a matter of moments before we will be spotted, cowering behind a broken crypt.

'Run!' hisses Linc as he blasts to his feet.

I don't need a second invitation. Panicking I rocket off after Linc, away from the torches.

There are yells from the Neville brothers as their torch beams jump and bounce violently all over the place.

'Saw one!' cries Lothar, as if he's just won the gold record of the year award.

'Bring him down!' yells Eustace. I have no real idea what that means, but I'm sure it's not pleasant.

Suddenly Linc has disappeared. He has turned but I cannot tell which way. All I can hear is his racing feet across the gravelly surface.

The Neville brothers start flashing again.

I take a chance and turn right at the first chance. Then left. Then left again. Now I have no idea where Linc is but I have a good idea how close the Neville brothers are when Eustace yells a warning, 'No escape Samson! You're dead meat.'

Lothar has a funny, little, gasping laugh.

I accelerate around another crypt—straight into Linc then ricochet into the brick wall of a derelict crypt. I hit the ground. It feels like slabs of broken concrete. Solid and uneven. I'm hurt but more worried about the Neville brothers.

I try to scramble to my feet as Linc hauls himself up by one of the crypt fences. I have a silly thought. I hope he doesn't damage it because he might get dobbed in for vandalism.

I can hear the Nevilles real close. And getting closer.

Suddenly the Nevilles fly around the corner, torch lights flashing wildly in every direction. They hadn't expected us to be so close. Now there are four of us on the ground amid screams and groans and a lot of swearing. I hear Eustace's torch tumble and crack.

Lothar hits the ground near my feet. I hear him cry out. Then he has his arms around my legs but they are not trying to hold me. I think he's trying to fathom out what's happening—and trying not to panic.

I manage to untangle myself from the younger brother before he gets his wits about him. Later I think that might have taken quite a while for Lothar!

By now Linc is screaming at me to run. He flashes his torch down a narrow cemetery lane and I have my bearings and I'm up and away. I don't wait for Linc. No use both of us being dead, but I just know he won't hang around.

We get through the gate and pause. Inside Eustace is swearing at Lothar about his broken torch, and looking for someone to blame.

Without comment Linc and I walk as casually as we can towards Rampart Street. Actually I am trying not to limp. When we hit the street we take a moment to check if we are being followed.

Nothing—yet.

We scurry across the street and hide behind the dumpster I had used as a cover earlier. It takes a few moments to get our breath and just a few more to realise that the stench will knock us out quicker than any Neville brother could.

We are about to take leave of Rampart Street when under one of the streetlights we see Eustace and a confused Lothar coming. They don't look like a happy couple. They look sore and sorry but I reckon I'm sorer and sorrier than both of them.

And I'm sure it's not the last we'll see or hear of the Neville brothers.

'Wonder what happened to the others?' asks Linc and I know he doesn't expect me to have an answer.

All I want to do is get out of these dark side streets as soon as possible.

CHAPTER 15

Sometimes on Saturday we don't do our act in the morning. Saving ourselves for the crowds later in the day is Dad's reason. Visitors to Nawlins usually don't come in until Friday evening and after a late night they have a long breakfast the next day. But some big jazz weekend is getting close so Dad makes a manager's decision that we should be out and at it.

I'm not all that thrilled because of skinning my shin getting into the truck and from the fall in the cemetery. But the show must go on as they say in showbiz.

Back in Royal Dad gives me a good once-over. 'What happened Xavier?' he asks. At least he hadn't asked it in front of Mama.

'Trying to catch a vampire,' I joke. 'Ever seen one?' Question for question routine.

He doesn't accept that ploy. He asks Linc the same question.

Linc is a bit more original. 'Tripped on the railway tracks while racing for the ferry. Didn't want to be late home.'

'Both of you?' asks Dad.

We remain silent.

'I think you are chasing up something to do with the emails and that crazy *Gambit* ad,' says Dad. It's a bit too close to the truth.

'I heard the Neville boys were asking after you,' Dad drops it real casually.

'Don't know what they'd want,' I mumble, as I tighten my Nike laces. I can think of a couple of things but not important enough to seek police protection for—yet.

I have a quick look along the street. No Neville brothers. But two police officers are ambling up our way on the other side. They stop and have a look in the window of the New Orleans Genuine Antique Store. One walks up to the doorway and looks inside. The other one, Officer Bell, has a good look in the window.

'Guess that makes two or three of us!' declares Dad. He's sitting on his crate and starts fiddling with the tape recorder. 'Might start with "Rampart Street Ramble".'

I always think it should be called 'Rampart Street Rumble'.

Linc looks at me and shrugs.

I think my dad knows or has guessed more than he's letting on.

Just as he's about to hit the PLAY button I see the two police officers striding in our direction. Dad sees them too and hesitates.

'Morning Officer. Officer Bell,' Dad calls out in a friendly way as the policemen stop right in front of our spot.

'Hi Dizzy,' Officer Bell says as he squats down to talk to us. 'Got a question or two. Maybe the boys could help us with an investigation we've got going.'

My heart misses a beat. I'm not a very good liar when it comes to straight answering.

'Only too happy.' Dad's happy to assist the police.

'You know the Neville boys? Lenny Neville's boys? Well, they aren't really boys now. More like young men.' The other, older officer looks at me. I don't know him but I've seen him around the French Quarter.

'Young crims,' corrects Dad, lightly tapping the PLAY button.

'There's been some talk and we want to get to the truth,' explains Officer Bell.

Here it comes. I've been found out for impersonating one of the Neville boys.

'Seems they got into someone's truck and tried to steal some farm produce. Need them for questioning,' he explains.

I almost laugh with relief but I manage to keep a straight face.

Dad pipes in before I can say anything, 'Haven't seen them for a day or two, but I'll let you know if I see them. Place would be safer with them locked away.'

I am sure Dad momentarily glared at me from under hooded eyes.

Officer Bell stands. 'Thanks Dizz. Appreciated.'

As the police officers disappear on their quest Dad starts the recorder and then stands saying, 'I'm getting me some coffee.' He often starts the day with a polystyrene cup of black coffee. 'You carry on like you don't need me.' Sarcasm New Orleans-style!

'You and your mouth!' says Linc as soon as he's gone.

'What?' I ask, all innocent. 'Won't hurt the Nevilles to get some of their own medicine.'

'And when they question them and they bring in the driver he's not going to confirm that the Neville boys were the ones in the back of the truck. He'll give the cops a description and that'll point the cops straight to us. Ever been to jail?'

'No, too young!' I reply but I think Linc could be right. I just didn't think it through. There's an ache in the pit of my stomach and it isn't gumbo poisoning.

We have a very successful morning and Linc and I head down to Bourbon Street for a break while Dad minds the store.

It's a bit of a surprise to see a small crowd standing where the Neville boys do their act. We go up closer.

Obviously it's not the quality of their performance that has attracted the crowd. It's the police interrogation of the star performers.

Eustace and Lothar are looking very indignant—and quite red in the face.

We move in closer but stay behind the cover of the crowd.

'Best crowd they've had in years,' I smirk, 'but I don't think it's a money-making show.'

The older officer who had spoken to Dad and us earlier raises his voice. 'You may deny it but we have it on good authority you were found in the back of a truck just after you left the ferry.'

Got him, I reckon. It's true. They were on the ferry. I'm starting to feel safer already.

Eustace protests, almost raising his fist.

Someone gives a little clap and Eustace glares in their direction.

Keep it up I will him.

Lothar has hung his head. Looks like he's hanging it in shame. That's more evidence, to my way of thinking.

'Think I'll put a dollar in their tip-tin,' I say with a grin to Linc.

'Just keep out of it,' warns Linc.

Suddenly Lenny, Mr Neville, stands up. 'Listen,' he says rather loudly, 'wherever you got that information, it is wrong! My boys never did nothing like that. When they got off the ferry they came straight down to the Bayou Bakery where we had muffulettas. Best in Nawlins! It's in the opposite direction. Must be a dozen witnesses down there! How many do you want for starters?'

Both officers look at him. Officer Bell takes out his notebook and starts writing the names Lenny gives him.

There's a frown on his face. I think he feels like someone is having fun with him.

'You catch who's been saying these things and I'll whip his hide!' says Lenny very loudly.

'If you are correct, Mr Neville, then we'll make their lives uncomfortable, believe me!' says Officer Bell.

The older officer nods his head seriously. My good feeling starts to evaporate like early morning mist on a bayou.

There's a gap beside me.

Linc has shuffled back from the action. A wise move. I'm beginning to feel things are getting out of hand on every front.

We get a can of Coke and head back to Royal.

'There's something not quite square,' says Linc as we sidestep past a row of balcony poles and some motorbikes parked against the kerb of the narrow footpath.

I do a hop and skip to catch up.

'I can't work out what part the Nevilles play in this whole mystery,' explains Linc. 'They are not the sort to be into big crime.'

'Petty criminals. Standover merchants,' I say with disdain and pomposity. 'Can't abide such people.'

'I think we should look at that ad again. I still have my paper.'

I nod in agreement.

When we get back to Royal we see the red pick-up outside the New Orleans Genuine Antique Store. Three men are unloading dirty cartons of goods and carrying them into the shop.

A man, I assume he's Mr Samuels, is standing at the front door like a sentry, watching the footpath both ways. He is smoking a cigar and trying to look casual.

'Could be the four diggers,' murmurs Linc as he tosses his can into a trash bin.

That would fit but we sure didn't see them up at St Louis No. 1. Maybe we left too early. Doesn't help to explain the encounter with Useless and Loafa.

Maybe they waited until we had all gone home and left them in peace. Had the place to themselves, except for the voodoo queens and vampires and ghosts and muggers and … I start to think the list is endless.

Different ideas appear to be occupying Linc's thoughts. 'Must check that ad again,' he says as he starts tapping away.

All I do is have a nervous look over my shoulder. I can just imagine the Neville brothers suddenly being within ten feet of our routine.

CHAPTER 16

That night, while eating some chicken pieces Mama had cooked, I do a bit of thinking. There has to be a definite connection between the red pick-up with Mr Samuels's name on the side, Winston Samuels's Property Renovations and Excavations and the ad. The fact that they were unloading stuff the night after the ad had required diggers is also suspicious. Not evidence, I concede to myself, but certainly coincidences. Especially the part about *four* diggers being required.

We seemed to have got the Friday part right. The next Friday was about a week away. I wasn't too happy about another excursion to St Louis Cemetery No. 1 again.

Night work seemed to fit in too if they were robbing graves—or, at least, doing something illegal.

But how did the Nevilles fit in? They weren't part of the gang of four—well, not when we ran into them. However, they did seem to be keeping tabs on us.

On Sunday there are lots of visitors in town. We make some good money tapping away. I always tap better when the dollars start to flow. Dad is happy.

Just before lunch Dad suggests an early break. Linc's follow-up suggestion doesn't go down real well. He is all for having another look in the New Orleans Genuine Antique Store. We are sitting on the pavement with our backs to an old wall.

I don't have any reply. I just don't jump up with enthusiasm.

A strolling Dixieland band goes past playing 'Ain't She Sweet'. A small crowd follows them, laughing and clapping. An older woman, in period costume, is twirling around under a bright umbrella.

When we can talk again I tell Linc what I had been thinking about our cemetery mystery.

Linc nods a couple of times and then says, 'I've had some thoughts myself. Same sort of things. I reckon we got some of it right and a lot of it wrong.'

I give him an inquiring look.

'Remember that guy with the tour group in the cemetery?' asks Linc.

I nod.

'Well, he said something that got me thinking.' Linc looks at me as if I'm supposed to ask what.

'He said the *cemeteries* were unsafe!'

'Remember that,' I shrug. I've lost the thread.

'*Cemeteries*!'

My mouth nearly drops open as I realise that there is more than one cemetery.

'Name some,' demands Linc.

Easy. I start with St Louis No. 2.

Linc nods. I have this sudden fear that he has them on his agenda.

'That's more dangerous than No. 1,' I protest. 'It's in one of the worst neighbourhoods in New Orleans. Storyville! They don't even do daytime tours there, I've heard. They'll cut your throat just to take your joggers!' I'm horrified. 'I wouldn't be seen dead up there!'

Linc grins, 'Probably only way you would be seen up there!'

I don't think it's funny and give him a mean snarl.

'Okay, keep your skin on! That's just one.'

'St Louis No. 3. That's okay. Then there's Metairie ...' I'm trying to think of others.

Linc prompts, 'Two up Canal Street.'

'Ahh, Cypress Grove and Greenwood. That's about it. I think.'

'Okay, Xavier, which ones should we try?' Linc can be persistent.

I suck air in through my teeth and make a decision. 'St Louis No. 3. Near the racetrack.'

'My choice too!'

Somehow I feel I've walked into a decision that Linc had already made.

Then I get a brilliant flash. 'We missed one!' I say excitedly.

I've got Linc's attention.

'Lafayette!'

Frowning Linc says, 'Bit off the main drag.'

I'm all excited. 'Where off the main drag?' I prompt.

'Up off St Charles Avenue. Get there on the streetcars.'

'I know that!'

'Washington Avenue?'

'Forget about streets! Where is it?'

Linc pulls his ear. 'Garden District?'

'Right! And what do gardens have? What do gardens need? Come on!' I shoot questions at him.

'Flowers?'

'And?'

'Gardeners!' He beams at me with what I take to be admiration.

'Of course. Of course. It's so obvious!'

I give a casual nod, 'When you know.' Then I'm all smiles.

The smiles don't last long. As we stand I see we are being watched. I don't know for how long but I suspect it's been for quite a while.

'Howdy boys,' says Lenny Neville.

Linc answers but I'm tongue-tied. I look about anxiously to see if his sons are nearby.

'Hear you were on the same ferry as my two boys,' he says quietly—and menacingly.

We don't comment.

'Bit of a coincidence, wouldn't you say?' he asks.

'Don't know what you mean.' I can't just keep myself from blurting the reply.

Stroking his stubbly chin Lenny waits a couple of moments before saying, 'I find that real strange. Can't say I like strange things. Don't like things that don't make a lot of sense either.'

'Where'd you fellows get to after the ferry berthed, is what I'm wondering.' Lenny says this real softly while staring at both of us and slowly shaking his head.

I shake my head with quick little shakes. It must be obvious that I'm scared—or guilty.

Lenny smiles and says, 'Well I'm off but I'll be around in case I need to talk to you again. Don't you go away now.'

I don't tell him that my feet feel as if they are stuck to the pavement. And I have this sinking feeling that everything is coming apart.

CHAPTER 17

We silently watch Lenny head towards Canal Street, probably to catch a bus or train.

My shoulders sag and I say, 'What now?'

'What now, what now?' Linc sounds like he's a record that's stuck on the same track.

'What now?' I shrug and do a little shoulder shake.

'Plan's unchanged,' he says simply.

'What plan?' I frown.

'Check out New Orleans Genuine Antique Store, dummy!'

I think we have been too close to trouble too often lately and I'm prepared to give it a miss. My reluctance is obvious. I am sure the ache in my stomach is going to cripple me.

'We gotta pass the shop on the way home,' says Linc. 'Might as well drop in. We just about got this thing solved.'

In utter exasperation I try to explain the obvious, 'We don't even know what we are solving!'

'Might next Friday.'

'Night!' I add.

'Still Friday.'

'What if those guys in the shop see us and recognise us?'

'We haven't done anything wrong. They don't even know who we are!'

'We were in the cemetery on Friday night!'

'No law against having a nightly stroll through a public cemetery. Besides, it was the wrong cemetery. Paying our respects to the dearly departed is what I say.'

I wonder what he's on about. Dearly departed?

I think of my sore legs and my fear of becoming a casualty of some witch or vampire—or the Neville brothers—or some graverobbers' hunt. 'I bet they are on the lookout for us. You can bet the Neville brothers have told them a thing or two.'

'I thought we agreed that the Neville brothers don't seem to be involved. They're onto something else.'

I'm not convinced any more but I've run out of arguments—or excuses.

'Don't worry. The store's full of shoppers and lookers. We'll be just some more lookers.' Linc heads off across the street. 'Make sure you get a good look at their faces.'

That's one way to give them a good look at us I think.

I follow Linc with a hunched back—I'm becoming the hunchback of New Orleans. Feels like I've got the weight of a coffin on it too. Just hope it isn't mine.

When we cross the street we see the three men with Mr Samuels and they seem to be sharing out cash. They are looking quite pleased with their share of some payment.

When we reach the storefront we stand at the window pretending to look at the display. It all looks pretty junky to me.

But I do watch the men.

Mr Samuels is better dressed than the other workers. I've seen him before.

One of the men is chubby. He has dirty work clothes on and is wearing a red scarf around his head. The other two are thinner and taller. One has his hair in dreadlocks and the other looks as if he's almost bald.

Abruptly they finish their business and manage to pile into the red pick-up on a raspy-sounding command from Mr Samuels. My relief is enormous. One less problem to face.

Not to miss a chance Linc walks up to the truck and peers in the back, as it begins to pull into the middle of the street.

'Another piece of the jigsaw solved,' he announces.

More like another nail in the coffin is my silent reaction.

'Truck had shovels and crowbars and other digging stuff in the back. Few bits of broken stone or concrete too. They have to be the diggers in the ad.'

'Can't imagine doing much digging at Lafayette!' I growl. 'It's just been repaired.'

'Restored,' corrects Linc as he enters the shop.

Repaired, restored, what's it matter, I think as I reluctantly follow him into the shop.

He is right, the place is full of shoppers—and lookers. No one takes any notice of us, but we still keep our distance from Mr Peter Moore and his assistants.

After a while of not looking at anything much Linc beckons me to follow him with a quick hand signal. He heads through a large arch to a back courtyard.

Here we find the cartons and stuffed sacks that Samuels and his diggers have delivered. The cartons are well used. Most are bound roughly with thick twine.

We look around the area for a few minutes then Linc bends down and tries to lift one of the flaps.

'Damn, tied down,' states Linc. That's what the twine's for I want to tell him!

I don't like all this prying in the open but I'm part of the conspiracy now. Bending down I pull at the twine.

'Keep an eye out. In case someone comes,' Linc hisses.

I stand and turn. My heart sinks. 'Too late,' I manage to say without moving my lips. An assistant is moving quickly in our direction.

'Can I help you?' he calls, but there's a threat in his tone.

Linc stands and looks at him and says 'No, we're just looking.'

'No use looking at that stuff. It hasn't been entered into the books yet. Maybe I can help with something on the shelves.'

'Just want something nice for my granny,' I say. 'She'll be ninety-nine next week. That's nearly one hundred. She hopes to make one hundred before she dies.'

The assistant raises his eyes inquiringly—or disbelievingly.

'She likes gardening and digging,' I say for some reason I cannot think of.

The assistant raises his eyes even higher. 'And you say she's ninety-nine?' he asks. 'You need a gardening store,' he advises with a fixed smile.

'Oh, I saw a truck outside with gardening tools in it. Thought you must carry gardening equipment.'

I have a quick look at Linc, wondering why he's not helping out. He can't. His mouth's hanging half open.

'Did you?' questions the assistant.

In the background I can see Mr Peter Moore looking in our direction. There's a look of concern on his face. He starts moving our way.

Now I start to panic. 'Must'a been going to another shop. I'll try somewhere else.'

I head for the front door with Linc close behind me. We manage to avoid Mr Peter Moore by going quickly along the far wall of his store, behind some really old wardrobes.

Outside and safe Linc says, 'What got into you? We should have been low-key. A ninety-nine year old granny who gardens! You told them about the truck too! They won't forget you in a hurry!'

My mouth is so dry I cannot reply.

'Rocket mouth,' Linc complains. 'You're going to self-destruct one day!'

He might be right but I was shaking too much to think about it.

CHAPTER 18

We played low-key for a couple of days or maybe we just managed to keep out of harm's way. I started to relax but it was probably the lull before the storm. The eye of the hurricane was what Dad said when things went quiet. In Dad's way of thinking that only meant that things had to get worse before they got better.

Dad still talks about Hurricane Betsy in '65 when the city was flooded. Before my time, then I thought about 'doing time'. Could be worse than any hurricane.

On Wednesday we got the next issue of *The Gambit* and found the ad. It was much the same as the earlier one but with minor changes.

★ DIGGER REQUIRED ★
Casual night work for four men
Successful applicants to report 17/24?9pm
No transport required
Part-time garden work at Underhill and Co.

I pick the changes straight away. So does Linc. The date for Friday, 10 had been removed. And it seems they had had a successful venture.

'They've done their dirty deed for the tenth. Now going onto the seventeenth,' says Linc thoughtfully.

I am not sure if he said 'dirty' for any real reason but I think it's a good description, though I'm still not sure what *the deed* really is.

He's quiet for a moment then says, '"*Garden*" is still in the ad. I bet they are going back to Lafayette next week.'

A ferry hoots a warning in the distance.

We are silent for a while before Linc continues, 'Need to start making plans.'

Sarcastically I mutter, 'Thought you had a plan!'

I can't raise too much enthusiasm. In fact, I think my face is fixed with a vague smile and unblinking eyes. This whole affair is turning me into a zombie.

'We'll do better than last time,' Linc tries to reassure me.

I'd like to say that it couldn't be any worse but I continue to stare ahead.

Charlotte comes in from the kitchen. 'Mama says if you don't leave soon your father will have to do all the dancing!'

I pout and think that would be a pleasant change, but she is right. We grab our gear and head for the terminal.

At the end of the levee path we pause and survey the commuters. There's quite a crowd waiting as the ferry pulls in.

'Can't see 'em,' I say to Linc.

He nods and we move cautiously up closer.

Still no sign of the Neville brothers.

The gates clang open and the few Algiers-bound passengers move off. Traffic starts moving and we board with the large crowd. Safety in numbers, I think to myself.

We find a spot near the rail and watch as the crew get ready to cast off. All the seats are taken by adults and little kids.

I'm about to heave a sigh of relief when I see Eustace and Lothar emerge from behind a corner of the ferry admin building.

With a shout, they make a dash for the closing gates, giving the attendant a big smile of thanks as they hurry on board.

It was a ploy—I know it! They wanted to be sure we were on board before committing themselves. Sneaky, is all I can think.

We don't move but watch the top of the stairs as the ferry swings out into the swirling current.

We see the tops of their heads before they disappear for a moment then they are on our deck moving straight towards us, gently pushing their way through the crowd.

I'm sure we are going to be knocked overboard. Have some terrible 'accident' and drown in the muddy waters of the ol' Mississippi.

Linc says matter-of-factly, 'Too many people here for them to do anything silly.'

I've watched too much TV to know that's not true!

Eustace and Lothar come up and stand with us as if we are old buddies. All smiles.

'Need to talk,' says Eustace. 'Get some answers.'

'Like what?' asks Linc. He sounds calm.

'Like, what are you two up to?'

Lothar repeats the question like a parrot.

'What are *we* up to?' says Linc, puzzled.

'Yeah!' nods Lothar. Great verbal skills!

'More like what are *you* up to?' I suddenly say.

That gets a look from both of them.

'We saw you up at the cemetery!' I accuse.

'You saw us. We saw you,' counters Eustace. 'You got something going and you're telling the cops it is us!'

'Cops?' I say as innocently as possible.

A couple of men nearby give us a dirty look.

'Whatever you're involved in we don't want a part of it,' says Linc.

Too late. If the truth be known we are actually part of it! In a big way!

'Us involved? We aren't sneaking around the town and back and forth on the ferry!' snaps Eustace. 'I got people keeping tabs on you two.' He's still all smiles.

'We don't go around threatening people either!' I retort.

'Just calling people names!' counters Eustace.

I don't have an answer to that but I get a look from Linc.

The ferry gives a hoot and begins its swing into the Canal Street terminal.

'I'm saying this once and once only,' says Eustace. 'You get us mixed up in any scam you got going and I'll start doing some digging and reporting! Got it? Get us mixed up in any scam you got going and I'll start doing some digging and reporting!'

That's twice I immediately think.

'Digging?' I cry. 'Digging! Who's digging? You're the diggers alright.'

Lothar looks completely lost. Eustace is puzzled. Linc has pursed lips.

'Always the smart-arse,' mutters Eustace, exasperated. 'Can't say I didn't try!'

The ferry docks and the crowd start to move off, Eustace and Lothar being carried with them.

Linc and I stay standing by the rail. I'm hanging on with both hands behind me. My knuckles must be white by now.

Linc moves forward and gives me a beckoning nod with his head. 'Come on,' he says. 'I think we have to rethink the Neville brothers!' He's toying with some new idea.

I'm not sure why. They still seem threatening to me. Probably even more threatening than before. In a friendly way!

CHAPTER 19

ate Friday afternoon we make our way to the Algiers ferry terminal.

'Not real sure the Nevilles are the problem?' says Linc after a period of silent walking. He's muttered that more than once.

I'm about to ask why but he continues, 'They don't really know anything. They've got no reason to lie to us. I think they were trying to call a bit of a truce—or something, the other day on the ferry.'

'Then why are they hassling us?' I shoot back.

'They think we're onto something, and want to be in on it. Then there's the certain matter of calling them names and poking fun at them. You do it all the time.'

I feel unfairly accused.

'Still, we shouldn't put too much trust in anything they say. We still gotta be careful.'

Mama would call that preaching to the converted. Mama can be a bit religious at times. Goes to church too much. I wouldn't trust the Nevilles as far as I could kick a honky-tonk piano.

As for being careful I'm wondering why. If we want to be careful, why we are on our way to Lafayette Cemetery for a night visit?

A shudder runs up and down my spine. Not a good omen I think as I take a quick look around for anything suspicious, like the Neville brothers.

We hurry to the ferry that has just docked.

On the upper deck both Linc and I have a look around the terminal and at the small group of passengers heading for the opposite bank. Neither of us let on we are being alert for the Neville brothers—but we both know.

'Hope you have good batteries in your torch?' asks Linc. He has his out and is testing the switch.

I pull a smaller torch from my jacket pocket and flick it on and off a couple times without comment.

'You call that a torch?' It wasn't envy. Looking at my bulging pocket Linc asks what else I have.

I don't say anything.

'You didn't bring food!' Linc accuses.

I look offended and say, 'Nah, just got my dad's cell phone.'

He frowns at me.

'It's a precaution. Might need to call the … police.'

'So they can pick us up for loitering with intent, or something. Come on Xav, you heard what the guy said in the other cemetery. They'll slit your throat for a cell phone.'

I hadn't thought of that, but I'm not giving it up. 'Never know,' I mumble.

We sit in silence until the ferry docks. It's still very light even though the lights of the city are coming on.

'Bit early,' says Linc. 'Think we should do a detour past the New Orleans Genuine Antique Store.'

I pull a face but Linc keeps talking. 'Just to see if anything suspicious is happening. Then we can cut across Canal to St Charles and pick up a streetcar.'

I grimace at the thought. I'm getting nervy. Reluctantly I follow Linc into Royal.

Somewhere in the distance a siren wails.

Passing the Sorcery and Spells Voodoo Store, that offers tours to places with documented hauntings—whatever they are, I pause and read the tour blurb that's in a window draped with black curtains. The notice is bordered with little black bats which are supposed to look like spooky vampire bats.

I just hope Lafayette is not on their tour list.

Suddenly Linc has me by the elbow and is dragging me away. 'Don't believe it!' he snorts.

Royal is getting busy with revellers, most carrying brightly coloured drinks, and as we reach the New Orleans Genuine Antique Store we find it has closed. There are a couple of lights illuminating the window display. By pressing our faces to the glass and shading our eyes from the glare we can make out the dimly lit courtyard at the back of the store.

'Looks all tidied up,' I offer. 'Cartons aren't there—unless they've put them in a storeroom out of sight.'

'Or put them in Samuels's truck for tonight's efforts.'

That makes sense to me. It all fits. Tidy up the area for the new shipment. Use the cartons again. They certainly looked like they were second-hand or tenth-hand.

'Soon see, one way or the other,' reasons Linc. 'Not much activity here right now. Let's go.'

That suits me. I'm sure we are going to attract attention if we stay here with our faces glued to the window of a closed shop. I follow Linc to the streetcar stop across Canal Street.

Within minutes we are rattling down St Charles to the Garden District.

Evening has cast its eerie shadow and there's no turning back now.

CHAPTER 20

After alighting from the streetcar near a bar-cum-laundrette that's playing music loud enough to be heard in Royal we dash across the road and make our way to Washington Avenue. I used to think the trees around here made the area scenic, photographic. Now they seem to be dark foreboding shadows and hiding places for any number of natural—or supernatural beings.

It's only a block or so to Lafayette Cemetery. When we reach it we wait in the shadow of an old tree and watch the entrance for a few minutes.

I can just make out a sign near the gate: 'Patrolled by NOPD'. I find that small comfort, but better than nothing.

I whisper, 'At least it's patrolled!'

'Don't you believe it,' replies Linc. 'They don't waste their time patrolling the places of dead people. They save their energy for live ones. It's a gimmick.'

I'm just about to make some comment like, 'Thanks for the reassurance', when I hear a strange rustling in the foliage above us.

I look up cautiously.

The noise stops.

But before I can focus on the cemetery and get my night eyes working, the noise starts again. Only louder.

Startled, I look towards the shadowy branches.

Something is definitely in the tree above our heads. I can see the dark movements of the leafy twigs.

Then I remember the Voodoo shop and I can guess what's waiting in the branches above our heads. Bats.

Vampire bats!

'Bats!' I hiss at Linc, pointing to the canopy. 'Bats!'

He repeats the word.

'Vampire bats!' I say.

He peers into the foliage but the sound has stopped.

'Don't think so,' he says but he's not very convincing.

'Then what?' I demand.

'Probably night birds. Starlings?' Linc suggests vaguely.

There is another sudden bout of rustling, which stops just as fast as it started. My heart nearly jumps into my mouth. Linc is hunched over as if Count Dracula is on the prowl for unsuspecting victims.

'Some birds!' I growl.

'Got a better explanation?' Linc retorts.

'No, I'm happy with bats!' I answer defensively.

I grab my torch from my jacket pocket and flash it up into the tree. I'm ready to run! The beams races around the branches making more eerie shadows than real light.

'Put it out,' orders Linc.

I ignore him but then the light catches a couple of small birds in its beam.

'Birds,' I say. I don't apologise and switch the torch off.

'Clear off!' I call in a voice that's a mixture of an angry threat and a loud whisper.

That starts the birds flapping and fluttering. There has to be more than two. The noise is like waves crashing on the shore.

An upstairs window can be heard being pushed open and a light goes on.

A female voice in a nearby room can be heard asking, 'See anything?'

The male at the window doesn't reply but calls to the general area, 'Clear off, or I'll call the police.'

I could probably handle that right now, I'm thinking.

Standing perfectly still in the shadow of the tree Linc and I wait for his next move. Probably the release of great growling ridgebacks from his front gate. They go for the throat.

Half a minute passes but it seems like ten minutes.

Then we hear the window being closed as the male calls to his companion, 'Can't tell. You never know, what with all those creeps and psychos hanging around the cemetery.'

The light goes out.

We wait a little longer before Linc says, 'Let's make ourselves scarce.' Even Linc isn't sounding as brave as he had earlier in the evening. But it was too much to hope for that he would abandon the exercise.

We stumble across some rough roots and broken path and make a dash across the road to the cemetery entrance, hoping that a police car—or a red pick-up—doesn't suddenly swing around the corner and catch us in its headlights.

We slip through the entrance and stand in the shadow of a wall full of vaults.

'Made it, safe and sound,' reflects Linc.

To me, that is the craziest thing to say. My heart is racing and it's not from the run across the road. Stuck in my mind are the words we heard on the other side of the street: 'all those creeps and psychos hanging around the cemetery.'

Safe and sound! I give a little snort.

CHAPTER 21

At night the white-washed vaults and crypts take on a ghostly, unreal appearance, as if they are from some dream fantasy. Deep shadows, dull outlines and distant, unrecognisable noises—growls, moans and thin cackles.

We wait quietly. We seem safe—for the moment. If we remain perfectly still.

I start fiddling with my torch. 'What now?' I ask in a hushed voice.

'Put it away. We've got to find a secure place to wait to see what happens.'

I feel like complaining that it's a pretty puerile plan.

Gradually my eyes get accustomed to the dimness of the cemetery. I can see it's laid out better than the haphazard St Louis No. 1. It has streets and lanes. A city of the dead!

The dead centre of the city, I muse, is how Dad would describe the place.

Some lights swing around a nearby corner and a vehicle comes slowly up the street, its lights making weird shadows in the nearby trees and illuminating the tops of some of the larger crypts.

We step back closer to some open vaults along the wall.

We don't move as the vehicle goes by, watching its progress past the entrance, from our secluded spot. Being so close to the ancient remains of real people makes me nervous.

'It's them,' I hiss. My heart is racing. We could be trapped. 'It's the red pick-up!'

Linc concedes that it was a pick-up.

'And it was red!' I assert stubbornly.

'Maybe.'

I move cautiously to the gateway and watch the lights disappear around a nearby corner, just a short distance up the street. I give a shallow sigh of relief.

'Could've been anyone,' states Linc. 'More than one pick-up in New Orleans.'

'Could've been the diggers too,' I argue.

I'm so busy staring after the tail-lights that have disappeared that I don't notice another set of lights swinging around a lower corner.

Linc grabs me and hauls me back to the protection of the vaults.

A police car cruises past.

'God, they're onto us,' I gasp but it goes on by.

Linc disagrees. 'Police cars spend all their time patrolling. It's their job.'

All the same I don't want to get picked up for acting suspiciously.

Linc begins to move down the wide, poorly lit pathway. I don't want to go further into this place but I'm sure not staying anywhere on my own.

I do a few quick skips and catch up. My torch clanks softly against Dad's cell phone.

'Ssshh,' Linc suddenly hisses.

I nearly collide into him before I stop—and listen. I can hear voices. Soft conspiratorial voices.

I listen but I can't make out any words.

I peer into the dark ahead, my eyes straining to make out any movement. Then I see the shadowy, vague form of two human shadows.

'It's the Nevilles,' I gasp.

Linc looks around desperately. We are by a narrow lane that leads somewhere between rows of crypts. He drags me towards it and we find a small wall to crouch behind.

Then we wait as their dark forms get slowly closer.

My joints start aching and I feel Linc move his feet slowly so as not to make a scraping sound, while searching for a more comfortable position.

The forms get closer and when they are just about opposite us they stop. I try to hold my breath. That doesn't work. I try to breathe slowly and softly. I swear my breathing can be heard all over Nawlins.

'Need a light,' says the larger of the two forms. Then I know it's not the Neville brothers. Strangely I want to laugh.

'Need some food,' says the second person.

They are not the diggers either.

'Good idea,' says the first person, but they just stand there as if they've got all day—well, all night. They are just a couple of locals taking a shortcut through the cemetery.

Finally they saunter off with some hushed whispers. I momentarily wonder why innocent people, if they are innocent, feel they have to whisper in the dark. Odd.

We stand and stretch our aching joints and breathe deeply. Too much is happening for my liking. Then I realise nothing has really happened!

We step back onto the main path and wait silently for a few moments, letting our eyes and ears get accustomed to the night.

I could be home watching TV—if it was working well enough to watch.

In the distance we hear a vehicle move up the street towards the entrance. It is obviously going slowly. We turn to the main gate.

Before the vehicle reaches the entrance the lights are dimmed and it comes to a stop.

It's a pick-up. That much we can make out.

Doors shut with a dull thud.

With only the aid of distant streetlights with their long spidery shadows, and the lights from nearby curtained residences, we can make out some feverish action. Several men are moving goods from the pick-up to a point just inside the cemetery entrance. Details escape us but these men are up to something and it's not above board.

The pick-up moves off, silently, slowly leaving some men behind. The lights don't come on until it's some way down the street. We see the canopy of a small tree illuminated for a few moments before it turns a corner and is gone.

'It's them!' says Linc. 'Now to find a vantage point to wait and watch for the action.'

I look at him with a feeling of dread.

My stomach turns. I've never seen a grave being robbed before.

CHAPTER 22

We sneak towards a point where we can hear the muffled sounds of men working.

We stay close together in the shadows of a line of crypts. Safety in numbers I think, even if the number is two.

Twice I trip over a bit of broken concrete or a protrusion from one of the structures. I manage to stifle any cries of pain or fright.

Suddenly Linc puts out his arm and when I bump into it, I stop. I'm just behind him but to one side.

'Down!' he whispers as he drops into a hunched-over position somewhere between a squat and being upright.

I do as I'm told without question.

We are close to the men who are working to some plan. Their voices are hushed.

We wait, straining to catch anything they say.

Someone drops something heavy and metal and I give a startled gasp.

I hear a man's voice snap a hushed, raspy rebuke, 'Fool!' then everything is absolutely quiet and no one moves.

Slowly we see the silhouettes of their heads above a small crypt about fifteen yards in front of us.

'Three only,' I whisper with its implied question.

'Other one must be in the truck,' suggests Linc without turning.

We watch their movement between gaps in the crypts. They are moving away from us towards one of the parallel paths.

Linc grabs my jacket and pulls me into a narrow alleyway that joins the two lanes. I wish I could switch on my torch to see where I'm going.

Passing across the end of the alleyway we see flashes of light. The men have strong lights with very narrow beams focused on the ground near their feet, but there's enough reflection to see that they are carrying large sacks and some digging tools. The last of the shadowy diggers has a couple of empty cartons awkwardly held in his arms.

Stumbling silently along the alleyway we get to within about five yards of the felons as they continue on their noiseless way. They are obviously men with a purpose.

And we are getting too close! I can imagine being caught, and hauled off to be buried alive, in one of the crypts or vaults. No one would ever think to look for us there! Joining the city of the dead before my time!

By now my teeth are chattering and I'm on the verge of panicking. If anyone said run then I'd be off and running.

I sense Linc's tension too and it is not reassuring.

The men stop.

Bags and cartons are dropped quietly to the ground. Digging tools are lowered more carefully.

A narrow beam of light flashes across the monuments and statuettes on some of the crypts.

It's odd, I think, to be looking at the tops of the tombs when you'd expect graverobbers to be checking out the earth.

'That one!' hisses one of the men with a raspy voice. Evidently he's the leader. The raspy voice sounds familiar. It could be Samuels and I'm afraid I might be right.

The beam of light settles on a statuette of a young girl. Suddenly there's a loud thud and the statuette tumbles to the ground.

'Bag it and pray to God you hit the base cleanly,' rasps Mr Samuels.

'Got it. It's okay,' says one of the other men and his silhouette disappears from view as he stoops to pick up the piece.

Samuels is in control of selection. His torch beam arcs around some nearby crypts.

For a moment it illuminates the faces of the other two tall, thin men. One has his hair in dreadlocks and the other looks as if he is almost bald. I know where I've seen them before. Outside the New Orleans Genuine Antique Store.

The chubby man with the red scarf must be the driver for the night.

The light passes over our heads and Samuels points to two or three bits of monument he wants retrieved.

No prizes for guessing what they are stealing and why, I reflect. They are not graverobbers at all. We got that bit wrong.

One of the men knocks off another piece of sculpture while Mr Dreadlocks is suddenly moving closer to us. My lips quiver and my throat goes dry but he stops on the other side of the crypt we are hiding behind.

For a moment there's no sound as if he's contemplating the best way to attack his task. Then there's a sudden deep crash as part of the front roof of the crypt is separated from its little building. Enough noise to wake the dead, I think, but I don't have long to think about it.

A piece of masonry has fallen away from the attacker and is tumbling down the crypt roof towards our hiding place.

'Look out!' I yell.

Linc is on his feet moving backwards and almost knocks me over as we turn and run.

'What's that?' yells one of the diggers.

'Bloody spies,' calls Samuels in a raspy, hoarse whisper. 'Get 'em!'

Torch beams dash around our heads.

'Saw one!' calls a digger.

'Cut them off at the gate!'

Linc and I stumble along the alleyway. Progress is not as fast as I would like. Above the violent drumming of my heart and pulses, I can make out the sound of racing feet along the wider paths.

Linc falls but he's quickly to his feet.

I hit my shoulder on a protrusion from one of the crypts and let a painful groan.

'Going to be cut off if we don't make a dash for it!' gasps Linc breathlessly.

That's all I wanted to hear. I'm exhausted already.

We turn into the main pathway and head for the gate. We have about twenty yards to go. Twenty yards to possible safety.

Suddenly, in front of us, in the opening of the entrance is the silhouette of the tall dreadlocked man with his hands outstretched. I'll never forget the way he suddenly materialised, a great black shape like Count Dracula looming over our heads. A silhouette of doom.

CHAPTER 23

'**S**plit!' cries Linc and I see him go left, then disappear into the darkness.

It's not Count Dracula looming in front of me. It's Dr Frankenstein's monstrosity.

The thing is bending down ready to grab me as I'm about to plummet by.

But I go right and low.

Too low.

I skid in a wide arc, across the gravelly path on my side, feet first, clipping the monster's shins as I go.

He tumbles in a black heap by the vaults, cursing and swearing.

Then the monster screams something but I'm too busy trying to find my feet.

Not a moment too soon because the beast is making a lunge for me. In for the kill, I suddenly think.

I roll to one side, then crouch in the shadows of the wall of vaults as he hits the ground.

A groan of pain and more cursing

Other voices are getting closer, louder and more menacing.

I've got to do something or I'm trapped and ready to be carted off to the Mississippi as alligator bait.

Putting my hand to one side to steady myself I feel nothing. My arm has gone into an empty, doorless vault just above ground level.

Without thinking I slide into the vault, feet first, just as a beam of light flashes across the path where I had just been crouching.

'Gone!' yells Baldy in a tone that accuses Mr Dreadlocks of stupidity.

I lie perfectly still for a moment then slowly turn over onto my belly. The dust is thick and the smell reminds me of something I can't place.

I can see out of the square opening at the front of the vault.

Suddenly I feel sick. I realise what I have done!

Samuels is yelling orders, telling his men to separate and cover the entrances. I'm not really sure how two men can do all that.

A torch beam flashes across the vaults, startling me. But I'm far enough back to be in shadow. My heart is snared in my throat and my mouth is dry and it's not from the dusty stuff I'm lying in.

Dreadlocks and Baldy take off in different directions. I can hear their feet pounding up and down the pathways. Every so often I see a torch beam flash across some distant crypt.

I give a thought for Linc. He must have made an escape, even if only temporarily.

Something sharp and thickish is pressing into my belly. Moving carefully to one side I slowly remove it.

Samuels is pacing up and down outside the vaults, flicking his torch on and off— muttering and cursing under his breath. I'm sure he's going to poke his torch and nose into my hide any minute now.

Bringing the sharp object up to my face I try to examine it. It's too dark. I run my fingers along it. One end is broken and crumbly and the other end is rounded, a bit like the top of a walking stick.

I'm tempted to sniff it but discard that thought almost immediately.

Samuels drifts past again, this time on the other side of the path. For a moment, I can see him, poking his flashlight into the corners and gaps around the crypts.

I can hear one of the men returning.

'Got away!' he admits, puffing.

Samuels grunts.

At this moment, I realise what I'm holding. It's part of a human skeleton. Probably an upper arm, or maybe part of a leg.

Only just controlling my breathing I count slowly to ten in my mind. I feel sick and scared. I try to think of something else.

'Don't think so,' comments Samuels.

His companion grunts a reply that I take to mean please explain.

'No noise in the street. And they went pretty quiet very quickly. They're in here somewhere and we've got to get them. Fast!'

The second man rejoins the group. I think it's Baldy. 'Lost 'em!'

'Don't think so. We just gotta be more methodical,' rasps Samuels.

'And hope no one comes along in the middle of it,' mutters Baldy. 'I'm all for getting out before it's too late.'

'We wait for the truck!' snaps Samuels, not encouraging debate or discussion.

There's a moment's silence, before Baldy complains grumpily, 'It's just that I'm starting to feel spooked.'

Dreadlocks gives a hmmph.

At that moment my dad's cell phone rings.

CHAPTER 24

I hear Baldy give a muffled scream and as he stumbles backwards, I see him through the opening in the vault.

A moment later he disappears, hits the ground and lets out another cry.

Dreadlocks swears fearfully, anchored to the spot.

Samuels is puzzled and sounding apprehensive. 'Shit, they're burying them with bloody cell phones now! Direct lines to heaven.'

I hear him move away from the row of vaults.

Baldy gets to his feet. 'I'm leaving,' he declares in a shaky voice. He's getting scared but I'm close to the edge of primeval fear.

'Stop him!' Samuels orders. He's talking to Dreadlocks.

Dreadlocks mumbles something like 'Dunno.' He's sounding spooked.

I see Samuels's dark shape stride past the square opening in the vault. 'We wait for the truck!' He flashes his light angrily at Baldy.

Dreadlocks follows, a few reluctant steps behind.

Opportunity has knocked. I know it's time to make a dash for it. I pull myself forward towards the opening, trying not to breathe in the dust of the deceased.

Cautiously, I look around the side of the opening. Dreadlocks is hauling Baldy to his feet. Baldy seems to have calmed down a bit. They are all facing, more or less, toward the main entrance. Something has their attention. I hope it's not Linc.

My heart is racing. I have to pull myself out in one swift movement, quiet as possible, then run.

Light from a vehicle driving slowly flashes. The truck is returning.

I hesitate. The lights are sweeping into the cemetery.

'Another pair of eyes to help find the prowlers!' growls Samuels.

The vehicle has pulled into the drive, at the entrance. Its lights illuminate the main path and a wide area either side before being switched off.

The three men move towards the now darkened vehicle.

I pull myself out of the vault, bringing a pile of grey dust and little bones with me. As I hit the ground I clamber into a running position and take off away from the men.

There's some sudden angry shouting at the entrance. I don't stop. Tearing around the corner I head as fast as I can towards the opposite end of the cemetery. I want as much distance between them and me as possible.

There are more shouts and curses from the men. Sounds like there are more than four. Reinforcements have arrived!

Trouble is, I had forgotten about the gear the diggers had brought to the cemetery. In the dark and being more concerned with escape I stumble through it, desperately trying to remain upright but I have too much forward momentum. I fly forward and as I go into a sprawl I ram into another being who lets out a muffled surprised gasp. Could be I've winded a mugger.

We crash to the ground in a jumble of legs and arms and cries of pain, each grabbing or pushing each other for support—or distance.

My immediate thought is that they have me. There is no escape this time. I can imagine being dragged to my feet with a fist just inches from my face.

I don't want to die.

There are more shouts from near the gate. I'm too distressed to care. I roll over, hoping to put some distance between me and my attacker.

'My leg!' cries a plaintive voice quite close by.

'Linc?' I say incredulously.

'Xavier?'

We laugh nervously in the darkness.

I reach over, slapping the ground until I touch Linc. And then I laugh a bit louder. It's sheer relief.

Linc laughs too. 'Just came out of that bit of laneway. Saw the car lights. Reckon it was getting too hot to be hanging around.'

I'm about to have a fit of the giggles.

Linc continues haltingly, 'And who should I run into?'

'We will have to stop meeting like this!' I gasp, trying to steady my breathing.

We try to get to our feet, hanging onto each other for support among the diggers' tools, cartons and bags.

We are making a bit of noise, so much in fact we don't hear footsteps quietly approaching.

Suddenly two bright torchlights are shining full in our faces. I can't see a thing.

'Got another two!' says a voice with authority.

'Just minors, young kids!' the second voice says with disgust.

I know it's not the right moment to object to being called a kid, but it riles me. Not that I'm in much of a position to be riled.

First Voice orders, 'Why you crims working for that mob?'

'Working?' Linc and I say together, shielding our eyes.

The men shift their lights from our faces to all the gear on the ground.

It's then I see that they are police officers. They are shaking their heads at all the stuff lying on the path, including two statuettes. Evidence.

They are the officers who spoke to Dad about finding the Neville brothers.

I don't like the way they look at us, all serious and suspicious. They think we are part of the digger gang—the great graverobbers.

'We are taking you in. Then we'll contact your parents!' says Officer Bell. 'This is more serious than you suspect!'

He looks as if he's very disappointed in us, me especially.

I understand exactly.

CHAPTER 25

At the police station we are accused of assisting suspected criminals—accessories. An older officer said he was tempted to make it a felony charge.

The digger gang are in the lock-up.

Linc tries to explain that we were really trying to help the police.

That gets some funny looks.

I have to add my bit. 'They had an ad in the paper for workers. I got an email!'

Then the older officer-in-charge looks at the ceiling and says something about destroying public property as he picks up the phone to ring our parents.

We sit on a bench seat against the wall and wait. My mind is numb. I'm covered in dust and grit and feeling very sore. I run my hand through my hair as a cloud of gritty dust drifts to the floor. I try not to think about it, *correction*, whoever.

I have a silly thought that I have an ashen face in both senses of the word. I don't tell Linc—right now it's not really funny.

Everyone that comes in looks at us sadly as we wait for the storm to break.

And we wait. I start thinking I'm going to have a police record before I'm old enough to vote.

Finally Officer Bell walks in, followed by Dad and Linc's father.

'I knew they were up to some caper,' I hear Dad say. 'Didn't rightly know what.'

Sounds like Dad's on their side. I guess I can't blame him but … family is family.

'Bring 'em over here!' calls the officer-in-charge as he picks up some forms and a pen.

We all make our way to his desk behind the counter.

The officer gets settled in his seat. 'Now, let's find out what was going on,' he says as he looks at Linc, then at me.

Dad grumbles, 'All started with that damned email, I reckon.'

That gets the officer's attention. 'Go on,' he says cautiously.

Dad starts to explain but he doesn't know the half of it.

I interrupt cautiously, 'I can explain.'

Linc interrupts respectfully, 'I can explain.'

The officer looks at Linc and nods.

Linc's father says rather ominously, 'I darn well hope so!' I can see he's thinking about some good ol' fashioned discipline even if Linc's taller than him.

Linc explains about the email messages.

'You still got those messages?' the officer asks.

I butt in, 'Still on my dad's machine!'

'Thought I told you to return them!' snaps Dad.

'Xavier kept copies,' says Linc with a shrug. Blame me, I think cynically.

'Good,' the officer nods. He's starting to be a bit more considerate. 'Go on.'

Linc tells him about the ads in *The Gambit*.

'You still have those?' the officer asks.

We both nod.

Officer Bell joins us. He says to the officer-in-charge, 'Those guys we picked up don't have a clue who these two are. That's what they're saying anyway.'

Dad sees the importance of this and claps me gently on the shoulders. A small cloud of dust drifts to the floor.

He asks, 'What's that?'

'Not anyone you know,' I reply cryptically, leaving Dad with a puzzled look.

After that things are very quickly cleared up. Evidently the police knew someone was damaging the crypts and tombs but were not really sure how or why at first. The Tourist Association suspected it was more than vandalism but couldn't find out why.

They also suspected that Mr Peter Moore was selling stolen goods, but were not quite sure what. Never quite put the two together.

Then it was discovered that Mr Peter Moore and Mr Winston Samuels were literally knocking off statuettes and other crypt ornaments and selling them as antiques from the New Orleans Genuine Antique Store.

At Lafayette they had been tailing them. After the driver dropped off Samuels and the two diggers the police officers followed the truck to where it usually parked while waiting to return later at a prescribed time to collect the thieves and their stolen artwork.

It was the police officers who drove the truck back to the cemetery while the driver was held for further questioning.

But it is our evidence that clinches the case against the raiders of the New Orleans' crypts.

Officer Bell says, 'You are two fine citizens.'

That pleases me, especially as we are not called kids.

He continues, 'Not like a couple of other *citizens* I can think of.'

I immediately know who he's referring to and as I'm feeling in a generous mood I say, 'Don't worry about the Neville boys. They didn't take anything out of the truck. Weren't even on it!'

Linc mutters, 'Motormouth!'

Officer Bell looks at me suspiciously.

Linc quickly grabs my elbow and somehow we escape the police station without further charges.

Linc and I become heroes of a sort.

Better still we get some reward money from the Tourist Association for helping in the capture and charging of the culprits.

I buy Dad a new TV.

Later we have a party. Linc's parents come over and some neighbours drop in. Dad cooks some chicken, Cajun-style.

'We have an old piano our Mama plays
While she sings "Bill Bailey come Home",
And our Uncle Ken plays "Basin Street"
On his battered old slide trombone.
Soon old Louis gets his trumpet out
And blows till he's red in the face

While big brother Will joins in with the rest
Playing slap on his double bass.

Sweet Georgia Brown who lives next door
Sings "Down by the Riverside"
As the Mississippi Steamboat floats on by
Full of folks just there for the ride.
Then just when you think we're almost done
Grandpa takes out his fiddle violin
And everyone joins in the fun once more
Till "The Saints Come Marching In".'

Suddenly I wonder who had been ringing on Dad's cell phone when I was in the vault. Guess I'll never know. Probably saved my life.

'Then I tap-dance the Louisiana blues
With cans clipped onto my Nike shoes.'

This story was in part motivated by a poem by
Elaine Horsfield after a visit to New Orleans.

New Orleans Party
We live in a town called New Orleans
In a house trimmed with old iron lace.
Most Saturday nights it's party time
And friends come to visit our place.
We laugh and play and eat our fill
Of shrimp cooked Cajun-style
While Daddy cooks up some chicken in a pan
Enough to keep us eating for a while.
Then I tap-dance the Louisiana blues
With cans clipped onto my Nike shoes.

We have an old piano our Mama plays
While she sings 'Bill Bailey come Home',
And our Uncle Ken plays 'Basin Street'
On his battered old slide trombone.
Soon old Louis gets his trumpet out
And blows till he's red in the face
While big brother Will joins in with the rest
Playing slap on his double bass.
Then I tap-dance the Louisiana blues
With cans clipped onto my Nike shoes.

Sweet Georgia Brown who lives next door
Sings 'Down by the Riverside'
As the Mississippi Steamboat floats on by
Full of folks just there for the ride.
Then just when you think we're almost done
Grandpa takes out his fiddle violin
And everyone joins in the fun once more
Till 'The Saints Come Marching In'.
Then I tap-dance the Louisiana blues
With cans clipped onto my Nike shoes.